# Has Anyone Seen Archie Ebbs?

Simon Packham

First published in 2022
by Firefly Press
25 Gabalfa Road, Llandaff North, Cardiff, CF14 2JJ
www.fireflypress.co.uk



A CIP catalogue record of this book is available
from the British Library.

1 3 5 7 9 8 6 4 2

ISBN 978-1-913102-72-2

This book has been published with the support of
the Books Council of Wales.

Typeset by Elaine Sharples

Printed and bound in Great Britain by CPI Group (UK) Ltd,
Croydon, Surrey, CRO 4YY

*For Lucy and Sam*

# 1

It's five past three on Monday afternoon. The summer term is only a week old and my life is so totally brilliant I want to chop it up and use it as a pizza topping.

Me, Josh, Amir and Caitlin (aka Top Table Productions) have just uploaded our latest masterpiece, *The Revenge of the Fruit* (Episode Six: *The Phantom Lettuce*) to our YouTube channel; Clint's made chocolate brownies for tea; and my joke about the man with a seagull on his head is going viral in the playground.

I'm Archie by the way, Archie Ebbs, the good-looking one standing at the front of the class.

'Thank you, Archie, that was really interesting,' says Mr Blott. 'So how about some questions for our Star of the Week?'

Chelsey has her hand up. 'Whose idea was it?'

Every Monday one of the class gets to be the Star of the Week. And you have to do a PowerPoint on something you feel 'really passionate' about.

Most of them are pretty boring. I mean, once you've heard one talk about gymnastics or guinea pigs with anger-management issues you've heard them all. But my subject is quite literally awesome.

'I'm not sure,' I say. 'I think we all came up with the idea at the same time.'

'No, we didn't. It was me,' calls Josh. 'Don't you remember? We were round Caitlin's house filming Episode Two: *The Tomatoes Strike Back*.'

'No way,' says Amir. 'I invented the whole idea of Awesomeopolis in computer club.'

Awesomeopolis is the awesome online city we've been building together since the beginning of Year Five.

'Well, who designed it?' says Jayden.

'It was definitely a group effort,' I say. 'Caitlin wanted the football stadium, Amir installed the streetlights, Josh designed a multiplex cinema with its own rocket launcher and I built the 24-hour Candy Floss and Pizza Bar.'

'So it was a collaborative effort then,' says Mr Blott. 'I'm pleased to hear it, Archie.'

Before we go any further, I should definitely introduce you to the best teacher in the universe: Mr Blott is a complete legend. He's got cool hair, he hardly ever shouts, and last term he guided the Parkside football team to the semi-finals of the District Schools' Cup. He's a great teacher too. I'd never really understood about 'place value' until he got the whole class dancing to his favourite Beyoncé song. After that, I don't think I'll ever forget that whenever you're multiplying, the digits move to the left (to the left).

'Oi, Ebbo. Got a question for you.'

The boy straining to punch a hole in the ceiling is another Parkside legend – but not in a good way. In fact, he's spent so long sitting outside Mrs Goodall's office that there's a permanent crater the shape of Callum Critchlow's butt in the chair.

'Yes, all right, Callum,' says Mr Blott. 'And well done for putting your hand up. But I hope it's a sensible question this time.'

Callum nods, but his toothy smile is a bit of a giveaway. 'Ebbo says that Awesomewhatdoyoucallit has got everything you could ever wish for. So where are the toilets then? And why is there no dog poo in the park?'

'I don't know,' I say, grabbing the opportunity to tell another joke. 'But it's funny you should say that, Callum, because I'm going to wash my hair with poo tonight. I've been washing it with *sham*poo for years. Just think how good it's going to look when I use the real thing!'

'Oh no,' groans Chelsey. 'Not *another* one of Archie Ebbs' jokes.'

But at least it shuts Callum up for two minutes. Because practically everyone else is roaring with laughter – even Mr Blott has a smile on his face. And I wish it could go on forever. Like I said, my life is so good I could eat it.

'That seems like an appropriate time to finish,' says Mr Blott, running his hand through his spiky hair. 'Now I know it seems a long way off. But before you go, guys, I want to remind you about the Leavers' party.'

A cheer goes round the room. Mr Blott has the *best* parties ever. Last year they had a chocolate fountain and laser show, plus Mr Blott filmed the whole class doing a wicked lip-sync video of that song from *The Greatest Showman.*

Mr Blott claps his hands and waits for silence. 'Because if you really want that inflatable assault course and the massive water fight…'

Practically everyone in the class shouts, 'We do!'

'…you're going to have to raise a bit of extra

money. And I'm not talking about the bank of mum and dad here. I want you to come up with some ingenious fundraising ideas of your own.'

Practically everyone in the class has an ingenious/silly suggestion:

'What about a sponsored game of Fortnite?' (Josh.)

'Penalty shoot-out – 20p a shot. Winner gets half the money; the rest goes towards the assault course.' (Caitlin – captain of the football team and the best player in the school by a mile.)

'Gymnastics display!' (The combined members of the school gymnastics club.)

'Cake sale.' (Zak, Jayden and the new girl with the name I can't remember.)

'I could do an auction of jokes.' (Guess who? Yeah, me, of course.)

'I could go down the seafront and win some money on the slot machines.' (Callum Critchlow – who else?)

'Yes, some interesting suggestions there,' says Mr Blott, looking quite relieved when the bell goes. 'Well done, guys. You've worked hard today. Let's hope you're all in the green zone and ready to learn tomorrow.'

## 2

We charge down the corridor, past the Modroc models of Anderson shelters and the recycling display, towards main reception. Mrs Goodall, our 'beloved' headteacher, steps out of her office to growl, 'How many times do I have to tell you, don't run!' and Mr Meston the caretaker (aka Mr Messy – not after the footballer, after the Mr Man) stares glumly from his secret store cupboard at the dirty footprints on his beautifully polished floor.

'Catch you later in Awesomeopolis,' says Caitlin, taking out the tennis ball she carries everywhere and dribbling it across the playground. 'See you down by the harbour.'

'Nice one,' says Josh. 'Maybe we could start work on the nuclear weapons.'

Callum Critchlow has just got my joke. 'Ha ha ha ha ha, *Sham* poo,' he cackles, helicoptering his rucksack at me as he charges towards his taxi. 'You're so funny, Ebbo!'

'Gotta go,' says Amir. 'My dad's here.'

I dodge my way through an army of parents and childminders. And there they are, holding hands in the bus shelter as usual: my sister, Izzy, and her six-foot-two, curly-haired giant of a boyfriend, Clint.

'Hurry up, you little melt,' says Izzy. 'We haven't got all day, you know.'

After two and a bit terms, her Year Ten makeover is finally complete: new onion-shaped hairstyle, new smartphone (I have to make do with a stupid one until next year), new vegan lifestyle, new taste in music (louder and ruder, but better if you ask me), plus a new superpower – the ability to change mood in the middle of a sentence.

'I'm going as fast as I can, Izz. But it's really hot.'

'Yes, we know that,' she says, rolling her eyes at her curly-haired giant. 'Clint and me have been waiting for ages, so get a move on.'

Yeah, I know what you're thinking. Why is your big sister still meeting you from school? Good question. But we've been walking home together since I was in Reception Class, so I guess it's kind of a family tradition. And at least these days I get to hang out with Clint.

'There you go, Arch,' says my sister's boyfriend, reaching into his 'Clint ♥ Izzy' rucksack and pulling out a sachet of Capri Sun. 'Get that down you.'

Clint and I have spent the last six weeks working on a new handshake. We bump fists and launch into the full thirty-second version.

Izzy grabs Clint's hand back and drags him on ahead. 'Come on, babe. Let's get out of here.'

I really like Clint. He's dead funny and he gives me all his old Xbox games. He taught me how to burp too. I'm not sure what he sees in my sister (if *I* ever have a girlfriend, I'll definitely check first to make sure she doesn't play the trombone) but Clint is obviously crazy about her. And don't tell anyone, but I'm really glad.

'Home sweet home, eh, Arch?'

We've lived at 22 Station Road since I was three years old. And from the hamsters' graveyard in the garden (Granddad made little crosses out of lolly sticks) to the family photos in the toilet, Izzy's drawing of Dinger as a kitten that's still on the fridge and the stain on my bedroom carpet from the unfortunate incident with Stretch Armstrong and the Diet Pepsi, I *love* every inch of it.

'Dinner'll be ready in twenty minutes, Arch,' says Clint, slipping on his special apron with 'REAL MEN COOK' on the front. 'Vegan spag bol followed by Clinton's bangin' chocolate brownies. I'll call you when it's ready.'

'Thanks, Clint.'

I grab Mum's laptop and disappear upstairs to my bedroom. No one's online yet, so I spend the next hour watching *The Revenge of the Fruit* movies. (Twenty-eight new views and six new comments – three of them from Callum Critchlow, none of which I can repeat here!)

Episode Four: *The Grapefruit Awakens* is still my favourite. Caitlin plays the ghost of SpongeBob and Josh drops rotten apples on her from his bedroom window while I dance round the garden under a white sheet to 'The Monster Mash'. It's probably one of Amir's best ideas, especially the slow-motion sequence, but the delicious smells floating up from the kitchen are so distracting that I'm really pleased when Izzy stands at the bottom of the stairs and screams, 'Teeeeeatime!'

Clint's a wicked cook. He's even made vegan garlic bread with olive oil for Izzy. We line up together on the sofa in front of the telly and get stuck in.

'What do you think of the new sauce, babe?'

'Good,' says Izzy, sucking up her spaghetti.

Clint waves the bowl of garlic bread at me. 'Go on, Arch, have another piece. But don't forget to save some room for your brownies.'

'Don't worry, I won't!'

Clint's always kind to me. But I can't help noticing that my sister is being unusually nice. She's scanned through all 203 recordings for my favourite episode of *The Simpsons* (Season 11, Episode 22: *Behind the Laughter*) and hardly even murmured when I snuck into her favourite spot at the end of the sofa.

But she's soon back to normal when Clint sneaks across to the cupboard and takes out the Xbox controllers. 'Fancy a quick game of FIFA, Arch?'

'No, he does *not*,' says Izzy, raising her inch thick eyebrows at him. 'And neither do you, Clinton. Because we're going to do our homework – *aren't we*?'

'Oh … yeah … sorry, Arch.'

'No worries,' I say, starting to pile up the plates. 'The others will be online by now.'

**dark_matter**, **joshmageddon** and **caitmeister7** are waiting for me in the harbour. I joined them as **<archenemy>**.

**<archenemy>** *Hi guys. Wassup?*

**<*caitmeister7*>** *Hi Arch. Have you washed your hair in poo today?*

**<dark_matter>** *ha ha ha ha ha ha ha ha ha*

**<joshmageddon>** *lol*

**<archenemy>** *So what we doing guys?*

**<*caitmeister7*>** *Build a witchtower?*

**<joshmageddon>** *Kill some zombies.*

**<dark_matter>** *Start work on the new airport.*

**<archenemy>** *Let's do all three!!!!!!!!!!*

But after we've built a witchtower and laid a bit of runway something rather weird happens. There's a knock at my door.

**<archenemy>** *Soz guys. Gotta go for a minute.*

Doubly weird because she never comes into my bedroom in the first place and, if she did, she definitely wouldn't knock first.

'Hi Arch,' says Izzy in a sickly-sweet voice that doesn't suit her. 'How are you doing?'

'OK,' I say, waiting for the usual sarcastic comment.

'Good,' she says, glancing down at my computer screen.

'Uh huh.'

'Looks quite … cool,' says Izzy, which is weird again because last time I mentioned Awesomeopolis she thought it was 'super-pathetic' and a 'total waste of time'.

'What do you want?'

She takes out a plate from behind her back. 'Clint left me some more brownies. I thought you might like a couple.'

'Great, thanks,' I say, grabbing the plate before she changes her mind.

Izzy starts to say something. 'Archie, I don't want you to get all…'

'What?'

'Oh … nothing,' she says, backing towards my bedroom door. 'I'm just going to practise my trombone. Hope I don't disturb you.'

I check outside my window for the alien spaceship that has abducted my real sister and replaced her with a chocolate brownie-bearing imposter. But all I can see is our next-door neighbour, Mrs Watts, putting a bowl of Whiskas on the back step for Bimbo and Margaret Thatcher.

So the big question is:

## Why is my sister being so nice to me?

# 3

An hour later, Caitlin's dad tells her to go and clean out Ronaldo (not the footballer, her angry guinea pig) and Josh and Amir decide they want to kill some zombies. So I run downstairs to see if there are any more brownies left and find Mum fast asleep on the sofa.

'Hi, Mum. How was your day?'

I'm not worried at first. Mum's a staff nurse in A&E. She often crashes out when she gets home from work. In fact, I've devised some pretty fun ways of waking her: tickling, water torture, waving my sock under her nose and once (but never again!) using Izzy's eyeliner to give her cats' whiskers.

But now I *am* worried. Because when I look more closely, I see that she's not actually sleeping. She's just sitting really, really still with her eyes tight shut.

'What's the matter, Mum, bad day at work?'

Still no answer. I cuddle up next to her and reach down the side of the sofa for the remote.

'I'll find something on catch-up, shall I? What do you fancy, Mum? Celebrity cake baking or psycho brides?'

At last, she says something.

'Archie, wait. I need to talk to you first.'

What have I done now? I've been loads better about not leaving mugs to go mouldy in my bedroom and I can't remember the last time I forgot to flush the toilet. 'It's not something to do with melted cheese in the microwave, is it? Because that wasn't me.'

Mum smiles. 'No. And it's really nothing to worry about. But I should probably tell you – so you don't hear it from someone else.'

The worst thought I could possibly imagine flashes into my head.

'You're not ill, are you, Mum?'

'No, of course not.'

Mum's tough. She has to be to deal with some of the stuff she sees at work. And apart from that rubbish film she makes us watch every Christmas, where the kids stop the train with a pair of knickers, I don't think I've ever seen her with tears in her eyes.

'So why are you crying then?'

She's also a terrible liar. 'I'm not crying. I'm tired, that's all.'

'Please, Mum. Just tell me what's going on.'

She grabs a cushion and holds it to her stomach like a hot-water bottle. 'A few days ago, I had a letter from Jerry.'

'Who's Jerry?'

'You know, Jerry, our landlord,' says Mum.

'What, the guy who came round when the ceiling fell down?'

Mum nods.

'What did he want?'

Izzy is practising Taylor Swift songs on her trombone. Mum pretends to be listening.

'Come on, Mum. What is it?'

She squeezes her cushion even tighter. 'He wants us out of here.'

I don't really understand at first. 'You mean, so he can do the decorating or something?'

'No, Archie, it's an eviction notice. He's retiring to Spain, so he wants to sell the house. We've got eight weeks to get out.'

I've seen enough rubbish reality telly to know what eviction means. 'But he can't, can he? This is our home.'

Mum wraps her arm around me. She still smells of hospitals. 'But it's *his* house, my love. He can do what he likes with it.'

'Does Izzy know?'

Mum nods. 'I told her yesterday. And just for the moment, she'd rather you didn't mention it to Clint.'

So that's why she was being so nice. 'OK … fine. But why didn't you tell *me*?'

'I just have,' says Mum.

Anger quickly morphs into blind panic. 'It's not fair. What are we going to do, Mum? Where are we going to live?'

It reminds me of the time I cut my head open on the dishwasher. I thought I was going to bleed to death, but Mum just laughed and patched me up with Steri-Strips. 'I don't know yet but we'll find somewhere else. We've got eight weeks, Archie. That's plenty of time.'

'I don't want to live anywhere else. I want to live here.'

'I'm sorry, my love. That's just not an option. But don't worry, I'll find us somewhere even better. You're always saying you want a bigger bedroom.'

'You'll never find anywhere half as good as Station Road.'

'Trust me, Archie. Everything is going to be fine.'

There's no one I trust more than my mum. And our cat, Dinger, obviously feels the same way. He's purring peacefully in his favourite chair. And, even though I know he doesn't like being disturbed, I can't resist going over for a quick cuddle.

'You hear that, boy?' I say, detaching his claws from the cushion before lifting him gently and pressing my face into his soft, warm fur. 'We've got to leave our house. You don't want to go either, do you, Ding? You'll miss the garden, won't you? And hunting mice under the shed and winding up the dog next door.'

But Dinger keeps on purring, as if he hasn't a care in the world.

Cats can be very stupid sometimes.

# 4

Six weeks later, I'm jigging nervously from foot to foot at the far end of the school field, while Mr Messy the caretaker and his crack team of helpers clear the track of hoops, buckets and bowler hats from the obstacle race so that the hundred metres can begin.

'You OK, Arch?' says Amir, waving at his dad in the crowd.

'Why shouldn't I be?'

'Dunno,' he says, trying to look professional as he goes through his stretching routine. 'You just look a bit … out of it, that's all.'

I've been trying really hard not to worry about our landlord's letter. Mum keeps saying that everything is under control and Izzy's so convinced that it's 'a lot of fuss about nothing' that she still won't let me tell Clint. The trouble is every now and then, it kind of creeps up on me.

'I'm fine,' I say, wishing I could just focus on the race. 'At least I will be when we get started.'

Luckily the last four weeks have been full of distractions. SATs weren't nearly as bad as I thought they'd be. Thanks to Mr Blott, I actually remembered what fronted adverbials were. Callum Critchlow was excluded for two days for 'accidentally' tipping the entire contents of a Year Five's lunchbox over her head. And the weather's been so lovely that Josh's dad took us down the beach for our first swim of the year in the sea.

'I think we're ready,' says Mrs Goodall, who looks dead weird in her once-a-year trainers and black leggings. 'Let's have the Year Six boys to the starting line, please.'

I've been waiting for this ever since the school trip to that art gallery when me and Amir had a race up and down the escalators and I suddenly realised I was faster than him. Every year so far I've been second. But this could be my perfect moment.

Mrs Goodall raises her hand in the air. 'On your marks, get seeeeeet...'

Well, nearly perfect. Mum can't make it this year because she's working. It would have been nice to have her cheer me...

'GO!'

Jayden shoots off into an early lead, but by the time we pass the gate to Mrs Goodall's conservation area, Amir and I have both overtaken him. We continue neck and neck until the halfway mark when I decide to make my move. Only, unlike in the race on the escalators, I can't seem to shake him off.

Amir flashes me the smuggest grin you've ever seen and starts to pull ahead.

'Come on, Tiger,' screams his mum. 'You're nearly there.'

I try to keep up with him, willing my tired legs and pounding heart to go faster. But deep down, I know it's useless. I might as well give up right now. At least Mum's not here.

And that's when I hear a familiar voice chanting my name.

'OH, AARCHIE E EBBS. OH, AARCHIE E EBBS.'

I can't believe it. Clint must have bunked off school for the afternoon just to watch me run. 'Go on, Archie,' he bellows. 'You can do it!'

And you know what, he's right. Somehow I find the strength to surge past Amir and disappear into the distance. Five seconds later, I throw myself across the finishing line and collapse in a heap.

'Well done, lad. Now up you get or you'll ruin my grass.'

The next thing I know Mr Messy the caretaker is pinning a first-place sticker on my polo shirt as the taste of victory explodes in mouth like popping candy. Like I said, my life is so awesome at the moment, I wish it could stay like this forever.

But I know something's wrong the moment I see them in the playground.

'What's up?' I say. 'Why aren't you at work?'

Izzy looks like she'd rather be eating toenail clippings and Mum's fake smile isn't fooling anyone.

'Well, that's a nice way to greet your mother, Archie.'

'Did you see my race?'

'No, sorry,' says Mum. 'We only just got here.'

Something else is wrong too. 'Where's Clint? I want to thank him for supporting me. At least *he* made the effort.'

'I told him I had a doctor's appointment,' says Izzy.

It doesn't make sense. 'Well, *I* don't have to go, do I? We're all going back to Caitlin's. It's vegetable lasagne night.' (Plus, I'm really looking forward to teasing 'Tiger' about the race!)

'You haven't told him, have you, Mum?' says Izzy.

'Told me what?'

Josh is chasing Amir and Caitlin across the playground with an imaginary assault rifle. 'Hurry up, Archie,' he says, unpinning an imaginary grenade and throwing it at us. 'My dad says he'll give us a lift.'

'We're going to finish filming Episode Seven,' says Amir.

(I'm playing the evil artichoke. I've only got a couple of scenes, but I'm pretty brilliant, if I do say so myself.)

'Oh, hi Mrs Ebbs.'

'Hi, Amir.'

If anyone should be playing the evil artichoke, it's Izzy.

'Archie can't come,' she says. 'Isn't that right, Mum?'

Mum nods. 'I'm sorry, Amir. I'm afraid he's got a prior engagement.'

'What prior engagement? You told me yesterday it was fine.'

'You know,' says Mum, giving me the eyes. 'That ... *thing* I was talking about the other day. Now, say goodbye to your friends. I had to park on double yellow.'

'But it's not fair.'

'It's OK, Archie,' says Amir. 'We'll do the scenes with Donald Trump's wig. We can shoot your bits next week.'

I try not to lose it in front of my friends but as soon as we're in the car, I really let them have it. 'You can't do this to me. It's not fair. You said I could go. You have no right. I hate both of you. Why are we going to the doctor's, anyway? What's it all about?'

And then Mum tells me where we're *really* going.

Afterwards I can't speak. None of us can. All I can hear is Mum sniffing and Izzy's thumbs pummelling her phone. And, apart from the boring DJ on the radio, no one says a word until we pull into the carpark.

‘I’m sorry, Archie,’ says Mum, scrabbling around in the glove compartment for some Pay and Display money. ‘I should have said something last night. But I didn’t want to spoil your sports day.’

‘I think I’m going to be sick,’ I say.

‘No, you’re not, Arch,’ says Izzy, taking her water bottle from her rucksack pocket. ‘Here, have a sip of this. You’ll be fine.’

I can’t remember the last time my sister put her arm around me.

‘Thanks, Wizz.’

And the three of us link hands as we walk towards the sliding doors.

‘Right, let’s do this,’ says Mum.

# 5

The only time I've ever been to the council offices was to buy parking permits. And we only had to wait five minutes. But it's at least half an hour before a lady in a black cardigan leads us through to her cubicle at the back.

'I've had a quick look at your notes,' she says. 'But perhaps you'd better talk me through it, Mrs Ebbs.'

So Mum tells the whole story again. But this time she doesn't sound like she's going to burst into tears; this time she sounds angry. 'It's just plain … wrong. I never thought it could happen to someone like me.'

The 'assistant housing officer' looks like she's heard it all before. 'This is very short notice, Mrs Ebbs. You should have come to us as soon as you got the letter.'

'Haven't you been listening to a word I've been saying?' says Mum.

The woman behind the desk looks almost as

fed up as I do. In fact, the only people smiling are the two children in the photo on her desk.

'Please don't talk to me like that. I'm only trying to help you, Mrs Ebbs.'

'Yes, yes, I'm ... sorry,' says Mum. 'Like I said, I never dreamt I'd have a problem finding somewhere. But rents have gone through the roof.'

The housing officer seems to know this too.

'And you're absolutely certain there's no one else you can stay with – a relative perhaps?'

'I told you. My mother's in a care home and my brother lives in Nottingham.'

'So you wouldn't consider relocating?'

'What? *No!*' says Mum. 'I've lived in this town for over forty years. It's where I work and where my children go to school.'

Even Izzy looks up from her phone. 'I've got my GCSEs next year. They can't make us, can they, Mum?'

'Of course not, my love.' Mum turns anxiously to the housing officer. 'So what happens next?'

'Well, firstly I need to make sure that you haven't made yourself intentionally homeless.'

It didn't sound funny to me, but for some reason Mum thinks it's hilarious. 'I've spent the last twenty minutes explaining it to you. What am I, invisible or something?'

'It's OK, Mum,' says Izzy. 'Everything's going to be fine.'

Mum's laughter magics into tears.

The housing officer pushes a nearly empty box of tissues across her desk. 'I need to make sure that what you've told me is accurate.'

'Why would I lie to you?' says Mum. 'It's not something I'm proud of.'

Mum's tears are obviously catching. Something wet and salty is running down my cheeks. 'It's all true, I promise. Mum never lies. Does she, Wizz?'

Izzy looks embarrassed and shoves a tissue at me.

'No.'

'Now, before we can decide that you're statutorily homeless, I'll need to see some documentation,' says the housing officer.

'I think it's all there,' says Mum, pouring the contents of the smart messenger bag she bought for her ward sister interview onto the table. 'Bank statements, wage slips, the children's passports – and there's my landlord's letter.'

‘What do you want our passports for?’ says Izzy. ‘We’ve got the Year Ten French trip. You’re not taking them away, are you?’

‘Certainly not,’ says the housing officer. ‘I just need to confirm your identities.’

‘Oh, for heaven’s sake,’ says Mum.

‘You said you’d find us somewhere,’ I sob. ‘You said everything would be all right. It’s not fair. You … you … you…’ I wipe away the snot and tears. ‘What’s going to happen to us, Mum?’

Mum leans across and wraps her arms around me. ‘I’m sorry, I’m sorry, I’m sorry,’ she whispers.

The housing officer clears her throat. ‘We’ll process your homeless application and let you know in writing within the next thirty-three working days.’

‘But that’s no use,’ says Mum. ‘We’ve got just over a week to get out.’

‘You’re supposed to be helping us,’ says Izzy. ‘This is a joke.’

Neither comment seems to do much good. It’s only when I start crying again that the lady behind the desk adds, ‘I can’t say for certain, of course. But, given your circumstances, you’ll probably be eligible for temporary accommodation.’

'And what does that mean?' says Mum.

'We'll try to put you in a bed and breakfast until we can find something more permanent.'

(There are loads of B&Bs down by the seafront. And the place we stayed at in Yorkshire was really nice.)

'Try calling in a couple of days, Mrs Ebbs. We'll let you know where we're at.'

Mum already looks happier as she pulls out her phone. 'Good. I'll take your number, shall I?

'We don't give out individual numbers, Mrs Ebbs. But if you call the switchboard someone will make sure you speak to the right person.'

'In that case we won't waste any more of your time. Come on, guys.'

The housing officer smiles at Izzy as she follows us out to the main reception.

'My daughter loves that game. What level are you on?'

'Do me a favour,' mutters Izzy, grabbing Mum's hand and refusing to smile back.

And just when I think my life can't possibly get any worse, there's a nasty surprise waiting for me outside.

At first I don't recognise him. He should be

terrorising Year Fives with his rucksack or sitting outside Mrs Goodall's office. So why is Callum Critchlow pushing a man in a wheelchair across the car park?

Maybe he hasn't seen me. I grab Mum's car keys and zap the doors. 'Hurry up, you two. I just want to get home.'

But then he starts waving at me. 'Oi, Ebbo. 'Have you washed your hair in poo today? Ha ha ha ha ha…!'

I keep my head down and pretend I haven't seen him.

'Oi, Ebbo. How's it going at school, mate? Are you missing me?'

'Friend of yours, Archie?' says Mum.

'No,' I say, jumping into the car and throwing myself onto the back seat. 'Never seen him before in my whole life.'

But when I peep out of the window, Callum Critchlow is still waving at me.

After a takeaway pizza and Mum's special hot chocolate with marshmallows in it, I go straight up to bed. I don't even check to see who's online. What would I tell them anyway? Two episodes of *SpongeBob* later, I close Mum's laptop and reach for the light.

My bedroom is the one place in the world where I always feel safe. Everything about it is perfect: the orangey glow from the lamppost that means it never gets completely dark; the vintage *Star Wars* poster Uncle Keith sent me for Christmas; a lifetime's supply of Lego in plastic containers under the bed; the swirly patterns on the ceiling that kind of look like Batman if you screw your eyes up; the photo of me, Mum and Izzy on Dragon Falls at Chessington; the mattress with the me-shaped hole in it; the poster Caitlin made for *Revenge of the Fruit* (Episode Five*: The Banana Awakens)*; all the Harry Potters lined up on the shelf.

Even with my eyes shut, I can remember every detail.

But I can't sleep. Not even when Dinger slinks in from the garden and curls up in his usual place at the bottom of my bed. In a few weeks' time this won't be my bedroom anymore. In a few weeks' time everything will have changed.

# 6

Mum once told me that 'love is blind'. Well, Clint must *really* love Izzy because he hasn't noticed that we've spent the last ten days packing all our stuff into cardboard boxes. Izzy told him that getting rid of most of your possessions was all part of the vegan lifestyle. And if Clint was at all suspicious, he certainly hasn't let it show. He didn't even notice when half the furniture – plus my Xbox – disappeared overnight. A friendly ambulance driver took most of it to the storage place in his van, and we stuffed the rest of our belongings into black dustbin liners and left them with an assortment of neighbours.

But Mum has saved the worst bit until last. And I only really believe it when she walks into the kitchen with the empty cat carrier.

'It's so not fair,' I say. Why can't we take Dinger with us? You know I can't sleep without him.'

'I keep telling you,' says Mum. 'Animals aren't allowed. I'm sorry, Archie, that's just the way it is.'

'But he's part of the family, Mum. We can't just abandon him.'

'We're not abandoning him, my darling,' says Mum. 'Like I said, it's only for six weeks. And I'm sure he'll be very happy with Mrs Watts.'

'Because she's a mad cat lady, you mean?' says Izzy.

'No, because she loves animals,' said Mum. 'And she's just over the road so Dinger will still be on his old stomping ground. Now, have you blocked up the cat flap, Archie?'

I felt so guilty about it. 'I used sellotape, like you said. But I still don't see the point.'

'Because it's kinder that way,' says Mum. 'And he seemed ever so happy. He was purring and everything.'

'When cats purr it can sometimes mean they're confused,' I say. 'I googled it yesterday.'

'Come on, guys. Let's get moving,' says Mum, her voice echoing in the empty kitchen. 'We can't put this off any longer.'

Ten minutes later, Mum has checked every room to make sure we haven't forgotten anything and Izzy's trombone and our suitcases are lined up by the front door. 'OK, guys, this is it.'

'No wait!' I say. 'I need to say goodbye.'

'You've already done that, my darling,' says Mum. 'You'll confuse Dinger even more if you go over there. Not to mention Mrs Watts.'

'It's not that, Mum. I want to say goodbye to the house.'

Izzy does that annoying new laugh of hers.

'You're not serious, are you?'

Mum gives Izzy the eyes. 'Yes, all right. But just two minutes, Archie. You've got school tomorrow. It'll take a bit longer to get there, so you could do with an early night.'

'Thanks, Mum.'

I open the back door and look out at the garden. I can just make out the hamsters' graveyard beneath the apple tree. 'Goodbye Adele, goodbye Chief Wiggum,' I call. 'Goodbye Tolstoy, sorry Rasputin.'

The house isn't the same without all our stuff in it. So I spend a few seconds in every room, trying to remember the good things that happened there.

KITCHEN: Spag bol and chocolate brownies with Clint, of course; me, Caitlin and the exploding chocolate cake; my terrible paintings on the fridge.

BATHROOM: Holding my breath underwater for one minute and three seconds; bath basketball; the wind-up submarine from Uncle Keith.

LOUNGE: Bristol Rovers clinching the Premier League on FIFA; the *Lord of the Rings* marathon with Josh; Mum's victory dance when she got the ward sister's job.

IZZY'S BEDROOM: I'd been banned from it since her thirteenth birthday party, but I can just about remember being allowed to play weddings with her Sylvanian families.

MUM'S BEDROOM: Opening our stockings on Christmas morning; hiding from thunder-storms; jumping on the bed.

And I'm fine until I see the stain on my bedroom carpet. I've tried my best to hold them in, but pretty soon my tears are mingling with the last remains of Stretch Armstrong and a can of Diet Pepsi.

'Hurry up, Archie,' calls Mum. 'It's time to go.'

'Just coming.' I dry my eyes and take a last look round. 'Won't be a sec.'

Mum locks the front door behind us for the final time and posts the keys through the letterbox. 'Don't look back,' she says. 'This isn't the end, it's just the beginning.'

Suitcase wheels on the pavement are usually a happy sound. You're either going away on holiday or glad to be home. But tonight, they're the most miserable thing I've ever heard. And no one speaks until we've walked to the other end of the street to find the car and jammed Izzy's trombone into the boot.

'At least we'll be able to find a parking space,' says Mum, tapping our new post code into Google Maps. 'At any rate, I think we will.'

*In 500 yards turn left.*

It feels like the end to me. Even so, I've made up my mind to keep my head down and not look back. The trouble is, I can't resist a quick peep at the old house as we drive past.

Poor Dinger is waiting patiently outside the front door.

'Are we nearly there yet?'

'Not quite, Archie,' says Mum. 'We're about halfway.'

'But it's miles. How am I going to get to school?'

Mum drums her thumbs on the steering wheel. 'I've told you. You'll have to take the bus with Izzy. It's quite simple. You take the number 4B into the town centre and get off at the library. And then you walk round to Primark and catch the number 27 right outside.'

'Two bus journeys? It'll take forever.'

'About an hour and twenty minutes if they're both on time,' says Mum. 'You'll just have to go to bed early.'

I haven't told any of my friends we're moving. I started explaining it to Caitlin, but I felt so sick that I only got as far as telling her I was really nervous about something before changing my mind and pretending I was having nightmares about SATs.

'What about my friends?' I say. 'How are they going to get there?'

'They won't want to come anyway,' says Izzy.

'You don't know that,' I say. 'Remember the play area at the place in Yorkshire?'

Mum's thumbs drum even louder. 'You'll have to bring them on the bus, Archie. I thought you said Amir loved buses.'

'Yeah, he *did* – in about Year One.'

'Yes, well, I'm not sure if we're allowed guests anyway,' says Mum. 'I'll try to find out.'

The other side of town seems to go on forever; past the posh houses at the top of the cliffs, past the graveyard, the football stadium, the retail park where we bought our sofa and into the narrow streets beyond. No one says a word, but I'm pretty sure we're all thinking the same thing. And it's at least twenty minutes before the Google Maps lady breaks the silence.

*You will shortly be arriving at your destination.*

This must be it,' says Mum, turning into a tarmac driveway that's dotted with weeds. 'It looks *quite*...'

'Oh my God,' says Izzy. 'You cannot be serious?'

# 7

The grey walls are covered in cracks and splashes of graffiti. It looks more like the carpet place that always has a sale on than that B&B we stayed at in Yorkshire.

The sign outside says it all. Underneath the words MANTON HOUSE someone has scribbled: Abandon hope all ye who enter here.

'Brilliant,' says Izzy. 'It just gets better and better.'

'It's only temporary,' says Mum, reaching into her pocket for the key. 'Apparently they can't keep us here for more than six weeks.'

'Six weeks,' I say. 'That's like the whole of the summer holidays. How can we…?'

The smell jumps out at us the moment Mum opens the door.

'Oh my God,' says Izzy. 'That is *so* gross.'

I can definitely smell takeaways and tobacco, but there's also a hint of something disgusting that I'm trying hard not to think about.

‘Where do you think we go for breakfast, Mum?’

‘It’s not that sort of place, Archie. We’ll have to make our own.’

‘So why’s it called a bed and breakfast?’

‘Never mind that now,’ says Mum. ‘Let’s find our room, shall we? It’s number 102 on the third floor.

We’re right at the end of the corridor. The black carpet is dotted with burn marks and seems to stick to the bottom of my shoes.

‘Well, that’s handy,’ says Mum, trying to sound like we’ve won the lottery. ‘We’re next to the bathroom.’

Izzy looks up from her phone. ‘What, you mean it’s not en-suite?’

‘It’s only temporary, Isobel,’ says Mum. ‘What did you expect?’

But I don’t think even Mum was prepared for what’s waiting for us behind the door.

‘Please tell me this is a mistake,’ says Izzy.

‘I’m afraid not,’ says Mum, looking round for somewhere to dump the trombone. ‘Well, at least we won’t get lost.’

‘Not funny,’ says Izzy. ‘That wardrobe is disgusting. And where am I going to sleep?’

'You'll have to share with me, my love,' says Mum.

'No way.'

It's the opposite of the Tardis: smaller on the inside. There's a double bed by the window with a single alongside. The ancient telly is about six inches wide and five feet deep and the armchair in front of it is sprouting white stuff like Grandma Ebbs' nose.

'Where's the kitchen?' I say.

Mum points at a tiny fridge with a microwave and a kettle on top. 'I think it's over there.'

Izzy is reading the fire regulations on the back of the door. 'I can't find the wifi code.'

'There isn't one,' says Mum, sinking onto the double bed. 'You'll have to use your phone.'

'I only get 500 megabytes. How long do you think that's going to last?'

'Well, I'm sorry,' says Mum. 'That's just the way it is.'

Izzy spews out a torrent of the kind of words I've heard a thousand times at school (especially when Callum Critchlow isn't excluded) but hardly ever from my sister – and definitely not in front of Mum.

The really scary part is Mum's reaction. She just buries her head in her hands and starts rocking. 'I'm so sorry, you guys. You don't deserve this. I feel like I've let you down.'

'Of course you haven't,' says Izzy, rushing to her side. 'You're a great mum. It's not your fault.'

I snuggle up next to them on the end of the bed. 'We'll be OK, Mum. And like you said, it's only temporary.'

Mum nods, but it's a while before she can speak.

'Yes … yes of course. Now why don't you two start unpacking while I pop to the bathroom?'

'Good idea,' says Izzy. 'I'm sure we'll find places for everything, won't we, Arch?'

At least Mum is *almost* smiling again. 'Well, it's taught me one thing anyway. I'm so lucky to have such amazing kids.'

Izzy's smile vanishes the moment Mum is through the door.

'Talk about the worst day of my life. Can you believe this? What was she thinking?'

'Yeah, I know. Dinger's never going to be happy at Mrs Watts' house – especially with Bimbo and Mrs Thatcher. We need to make sure he's OK.'

'Never mind that,' says Izzy, grabbing my wrist. 'You've got to promise me something, Archie.'

'What?'

Her grip tightens. 'Promise you won't tell anyone.'

'Tell anyone what?'

'Don't be an idiot. That we're living in this dump, of course. Swear to me that you won't breathe a word to your friend Caitlin or that weird kid who likes buses.'

'But why?

'Are you stupid or something, Archie? Do you honestly want your friends to know?'

It does kind of make sense. Manton House isn't exactly the kind of place you'd want to invite your mates for a sleepover. 'What shall I tell them?'

'Say we're having building work or something. You heard Mum. We'll only be here for six weeks. You won't have to keep it up for long.'

'I don't know,' I say, remembering what a bad liar I am. 'Wouldn't it be better to...?

'Just swear, OK? I can't have anyone at school finding out about this.'

I know better than anyone what my sister is

capable of. 'All right, I swear. But when are you going to tell Clint?'

'Like, never,' says Izzy, practically puking as she takes a quick peep in the fridge. 'And you can't tell him either.'

'But he'll find out tomorrow when he comes back with us.'

'No, he won't. Station Road was bad enough, but it'll be the end of everything if he ever comes here.'

'Clint won't care, Izzy. You should tell him.'

'You're joking, aren't you? Please, Archie. This is really important. You don't know what secondary school is like.'

Izzy's right. Back in the good old days, starting at St Thomas's Community College was practically the only thing I ever worried about. 'Yeah … OK. I'm just rubbish at lying, that's all.'

'Don't worry, Arch. I'll work out something to say to him. Just make sure you keep your mouth shut.'

Watching TV in bed seemed like a fun idea to start with. But it turns out we can only get one channel and the 'Live Jewellery Auction' isn't nearly as exciting as Debs and Abby think.

'That's quite enough of that,' says Mum, walking all the way to the telly because there isn't a remote. 'I've got an early start tomorrow and you two need to make sure you're ready for the bus.'

'It's not even ten o clock,' says Izzy.

'Please,' says Mum. 'Can we not argue about this? I've got enough to think about as it is.' She climbs back into bed and clicks off the wonky table light. Her voice is pretty wonky too. 'Sleep well.'

'Night, Mum.'

But the paper-thin curtains are no match for the security lights, my new bed has a Grand Canyon-sized trench in the middle and trying to sleep with my sister's head about six inches away from me is practically impossible.

Maybe it was the Pepsi and the microwave pizza. Or maybe it's just the heat. But all I can do is lie awake worrying. Can we really live like this for six whole weeks? How's Mum going to make me a cake if we're still here for my birthday? How can I possibly keep it a secret from all my friends?'

At least when Caitlin texts to ask why I'm not online, I can tell her the truth:

*No internet. See you tomorrow.*

# 8

By the end of Monday afternoon, I can't fight it anymore. Chelsey's Star of the Week talk (about her 'amazing' collection of sugar sachets) is so boring that I must have fallen asleep.

'I hope we're not keeping you awake, Archie?'

But it's not Mr Blott's voice that makes me jump. It's the sound of twenty-five of my classmates laughing their heads off and Callum Critchlow poking me in the ribs with his reading diary.

'What … eh … who's there?'

'It's the Honey Monster,' says Callum, cackling with glee.

I'm terrified the smell will give me away. No matter how many times I've washed myself in the boys' toilets, the stink of the B&B seems to follow me around like an unwanted invisible friend. That's why I've been keeping my distance from Josh, Amir and Caitlin.

At least my favourite teacher is still smiling.

'Been up all night playing video games, have we, Archie?'

Well, how can I tell him the truth? That after two horrible bus journeys and a long sleepless night in a bed and breakfast for the 'statutorily' homeless, I'm completely exhausted. 'Yes, Mr Blott.'

'No, you weren't,' says Caitlin. 'You said your internet was down.'

'He probably had the runs,' says Josh. 'He's been running to the bog all day.'

I could normally think of a funny comeback. But I'm so tired I just want to curl up on the table and go to sleep. 'No … I … I…'

'Well, I hope you've got the energy for athletics club,' says Mr Blott.

It's practically a two-hour bus journey and Izzy said she had no intention of hanging around to watch a bunch of kids running round the school field. 'I'm sorry, Mr Blott. I can't make it tonight.'

'But we've got the District Sports coming up,' says Caitlin. 'What's the matter with you?'

I kind of want to say something about Manton House. But somehow, I manage not to crack. 'Nothing, it's just … you know … it's just…'

Perhaps Mr Blott has seen the tear in my eye. 'That's fine, Archie. Don't worry about it. We'll see you next week.' He claps his hands and turns to the rest of the class. 'OK, guys. You'll be sad to hear that that's all we've got time for.'

And after a few sarcastic 'aahs' the stampede for the cloakroom begins.

They're waiting for me by the bus shelter as usual. But for the first time I can remember, they're not holding hands.

'All right, Arch?'

I offer Clint my fist, but for some reason he doesn't bump it. 'Yeah … fine, thanks.'

'The bus will be here soon,' says Izzy. 'You might as well go, Clint.'

'What's the matter, babe? Have I done something wrong?'

Izzy turns away from him, burying her hands in her blazer pockets. 'No, course not.'

If Clint was a cat he would probably be purring by now. 'I don't get it, Izzer. Mum'll pick me up wherever it is.'

'I told you,' says Izzy. 'We've got the decorators in. I don't want you seeing it until it's ready.'

'This is me you're talking to, babe. Do you really think I'm bothered about the colour scheme?' He turns to me with a friendly grin. 'So what's the new crib like, Archie – sounds bangin'?'

'Well, it's hard to—'

'You know what it's like,' says Izzy. 'All houses look the same. Don't they, Archie?'

She's giving me the eyes. I haven't got much choice. 'Er … yeah.'

Clint has taken out his phone. 'What did you say the address was, babe?'

'I didn't,' says Izzy. 'Like I told you, it's *kind* of past the seafront and *quite* near the cliffs. I'll give you the address when the decorators have gone.' The bus is waiting at the traffic lights. She kisses Clint on the cheek and steps forward to meet it. 'See you in PSHE.'

'*No*,' says Clint, who usually goes along with everything Izzy says. 'I don't care about the stupid decorating. I love you, Izzy, and I'm coming with you.'

'You can't,' she says, her voice all cracked and teary. 'I'm sorry, C. I just don't want you to.'

'Please, babe.' He waves his 'Clint ♥ Izzy'

rucksack at her. 'I've got the ingredients for vegan chilli con carne.'

What's she playing at? I *have* to say something. 'Come on, Wizz. Why don't you tell him the real reason?'

'Right, yeah, I will.' The bus is pulling away from the traffic lights. Izzy seems to think forever. 'The truth is … the truth is… I didn't want to hurt your feelings. But…'

'But what?' says Clint.'

Her eyes never leave the blob of chewing gum on the pavement. 'You can't come back with us because … because…'

'What?'

'Because I've got a new boyfriend,' says Izzy. 'I can't be with you anymore, Clinton. I'm seeing someone else.'

Clint lets out a howl of pain. 'It's not Aidan Foden, is it?'

'It's no one from school,' says Izzy hastily. 'It's just a guy I met at the trombone workshop.'

And suddenly I feel this uncontrollable urge to scratch. The red blotches that appeared on my arms in the middle of mental maths feel like they're on fire.

'I don't believe you,' says Clint, tugging at his curly hair. 'Why are you being like this?'

I can't believe it either. Clint is about the best thing that's happened to our family in ages. 'She doesn't mean it. I know she doesn't.'

The bus doors open and Izzy drags me up the steps. 'Yes, I do,' she says. 'You're dumped, Clint. End of.'

'This is all wrong,' I say, scratching and crying at the same time.

'It's OK, Archie,' says Clint. 'Don't you worry. This isn't over. I'll do whatever it takes, babe. But I'm telling you now, I'm going to get you back it it's the last thing I—'

The doors close and the bus pulls away.

# 9

Izzy's still crying when we get off outside Primark. But she stops suddenly when she sees a bunch of girls from her school waiting in the bus shelter by the library.

'That's all I needed,' she says, pushing me towards the shopping mall. 'We'll have to get the next one.'

I'm already really angry with her. How could she do that to Clint? 'But there isn't another one for half an hour. And it's getting late.'

'Why, what's the matter?' she says. 'Desperate to get "home", are you?'

I've been trying to blot it out of my mind. The thought of another night in the B&B is unbearable. 'No. But I could have gone to athletics practice.'

'Yeah, sorry about that,' says Izzy, sounding almost like she means it. 'But if Courtney Foden finds out where I'm living it'll be all over Year Ten like a rash.'

That's enough to start me scratching again. 'So what are we going to do?'

She scrabbles around in the front of her rucksack for some change. 'We could get a drink if you like.'

A few minutes later we're sharing a Diet Coke in the food court.

'You OK, Arch?' says Izzy, tapping on the shiny table with her purple fingernails. 'You can tell me you know.'

Things must be bad if my sister's being nice to me. 'I'm worried about Dinger. What if he's really unhappy there? Why don't we go back and check?'

'He'll be fine,' says Izzy, checking Burger King for random Year Tens.

'And I still don't understand why you dumped Clint. I thought you really liked him.'

'I do.'

'And you … you haven't got a new boyfriend, have you?'

Izzy laughs. 'Course not. But I had to tell him something or he would have followed us all the way back.'

'So what?'

'Look, how many times do I have to say this,

Archie? No one can know about it – especially not Clint. And if you even think of telling him, you're dead. Do you understand?'

I nod and suck up the last dregs of ice. 'I won't have to, anyway. He'll soon work out you're making it all up.'

'It's only for six weeks,' says Izzy. 'We'll just have to be careful, that's all.'

'Remember how Mum used to take us on the cliffs to fly our kite?'

I'm far too busy thinking about Dinger to remember the good old days.

'Dunno, suppose so.'

'You loved it,' says Izzy, as the bus struggles up the hill from the seafront. 'Even when you were little "Anxious Archie".'

That was years ago. I wish she wouldn't still call me that.

'If you say so.'

'It's so chilled up there,' says Izzy, pressing her nose to the window. 'It's like the perfect place for a romantic date.'

And now she's crying again.

'Cheer up, Wizz. It's not the end of the world, is it?'

'Isn't it?'

Halfway to the top of the cliffs I get Amir's text: *sleepover at mine on Saturday. Josh's bringing COD.* The thought of a sleepless night on Amir's floor with Josh's smelly feet in my face really cheers me up for a minute.

'Who's texting you anyway,' sniffs Izzy.

'It's Amir. There's a sleepover at his place on Saturday.'

'You know you can't go, don't you?'

'Why not?'

Izzy flashes me her 'isn't Archie stupid?' face. 'You know how it works. If you went to Amir's you'd have to invite him back to Manton House. And that can *never* happen. Do you understand?

And then I realise what it means. 'Wait. Are you saying I've got turn down every single invitation for the next *six* weeks?'

Izzy nods.

'But that's ages!'

'Exactly,' says Izzy. So you'd better start working on your excuses, hadn't you?'

And I'm trying to decide between a road trip to Uncle Keith's and a gala evening of trombone music when Izzy jumps up and pushes the bell.

'Right, come on, Archie. This is our stop.'

'No, it's not. It's miles yet.'

'I don't care,' says Izzy, dragging me out of my seat. 'I've had an idea.'

'But the next one's not for half an hour. And Mum said she'd try to get back early.'

'I'm not arguing with you, Archie. Get off the bus!'

'Go and stand in front of the gate, Archie.'

'What for?'

Izzy takes out her phone. 'So I can take some photos.'

A sea breeze is blowing up and I'm starting to get hungry. 'Why?'

'Because I say so.'

It's obviously bin night. A platoon of blue wheelie bins stands guard over the posh cars in the massive driveways. 'Not until you tell me what we're doing here.'

'This is just phase one,' she says, looking really pleased with herself. 'Let's give that Courtney Foden something to talk about.'

And I'm so confused that I probably start purring. 'What are you going to do?'

'I'm going to Snapchat the photos of our new house to everyone who matters in Year Ten.' She points her phone at me. 'I bet there's a lovely sea view from your bedroom.'

'Wait a minute. You're not saying you're going to pretend this is our new house?'

'Not just this one,' says Izzy. 'Some know-it-all might recognise it. We'll take photos of a couple and kind of pick 'n' mix. Go on, smile.'

And it's almost fun for a while; walking from house to house taking silly photos of ourselves. At least it takes my mind off where we'll be spending the night. But then Izzy sees the house with the 'Sold' sign.

'This one's perfect, Arch.' (It's more modern than the others with lots of glass.) 'And there are no bins out the front, so it's obviously empty.'

'Do we have to? The bus will be here soon.'

'We've got eight minutes,' says Izzy, putting her head down and unbolting the gate. 'Come on, follow me.'

We creep down the alley along the side of the house. 'Please, Wizz. I don't think we should—'

'Wow. That is … a*maz*ing,' says my sister. 'In your face, Courtney.'

My mouth falls open like a gobsmacked goldfish. 'But it's *so*…'

The garden seems to go on forever. In the centre of the freshly mowed lawn is a giant oak tree (at least, I think it's an oak tree) surrounded by a life-sized family of metal statues flying kites; Mum, Dad, three children and a shaggy dog. What family wouldn't be happy in a place like this?

'I wish Mum could see this place,' I say, starting to feel sad again. 'She'd love it.'

'Well, she can't, can she? And you'd better not tell her about it.'

'How many bedrooms do you think there are – six, seven?'

Izzy is taking some shots of the garden. 'Wait a minute. It's not, is it?'

'Not *what*?'

'Over there, in the corner. We so have to get a picture of that.'

Apart from a few puddles, the L-shaped

swimming pool is completely empty. We take it in turns to lie on the wooden loungers and pretend to be sunbathing.

And then Izzy has an idea. 'Go on, Archie, get in.'

'What about the bus?'

'We've still got time. Come on, it'll be a laugh.'

I inch down the ladder and lower myself into the deep end. 'What do I do now?'

'Pretend to be swimming,' she says. 'Yeah, that's good. One more photo and then we're—'

'Hello, *hello*?' says a voice. 'Anybody there?'

'Quick,' says Izzy. 'Someone's coming.'

But I can't seem to get a grip on the ladder. 'It's no good I—'

'Hurry up!'

There's no water, but it still feels like I'm drowning. And by the time I've managed to drag myself to safety, my lungs are bursting. 'Now what?'

'Hide,' says Izzy.

I was always pretty rubbish at this game. Ask Amir. Izzy finds a perfect place in the bushes. I crouch behind the smiling Buddha who's meditating at the poolside. The trouble is, I'm about six inches taller than the statue and half my head is sticking out.

'I'm warning you,' said the voice. 'If you don't come out now, I'm going to call the police.'

'Stay where you are,' whispers Izzy.

An old man in a green waxed jacket is stumbling across the lawn towards us. 'This is private property. Do you understand?'

'You heard him,' I hiss. 'He's going to call the police.'

'He's bluffing,' whispers Izzy. 'Keep quiet and *don't* panic.' (It's all right for her. She's found a nice safe place in the bushes.)

The old man steps onto the wooden decking surrounding the pool. I hold my breath, while he gasps for his. 'I suppose you think this is funny. Well, let me tell you something, it's not.'

But I'm certainly not laughing when he checks behind the giant flowerpots, bends creakily to inspect beneath the wooden loungers and totters slowly towards the deep end.

'Come out … come out … wherever you are.'

My heart belly flops into my mouth as the old man gets warmer … and warmer … and warmer, until he's so close I can even smell his dark-brown shoe polish and his sickly butterscotch breath. In fact, if I hadn't just closed my eyes, I'd probably be staring straight at him.

Two beads of sweat start racing down my back as I search desperately for a believable explanation. But 'I'm sorry, I think I must have got lost' is totally pathetic. And how many ten-year-old Amazon delivery drivers do *you* know?

So why doesn't he say something? If he's trying to scare me, he's wasting his time because I couldn't be more terrified than I am already. But when I open my eyes, just the tinniest chink, I see something so weird that it doesn't make sense.

The old man takes out a phone the size of a toasted cheese sandwich and starts dialling.

'It's all right, Angela, they've gone. Yes, just kids again, I think.' He turns back towards the house. 'Put the kettle on and I'll be with you in a tick.'

And I'm still paralysed with a mixture of fear and amazement when Izzy steps out of the bushes with a big smile on her face. 'Well, that was lucky.'

I steady myself on the smiling Buddha. 'What … just … happened? Why didn't he see me, Wizz?'

'Well, it's obvious, isn't it?'

'Is it?'

'Should have gone to Specsavers, shouldn't he? The poor old bloke's as blind as a bat.'

'Are you ... sure?' I say, still trying to make sense of it all. 'How could he be if he dialled that number?'

Izzy's American accent is almost as annoying as her new laugh. 'Oh, so you've got a new superpower, have you? Mild-mannered Archie Ebbs is *Invisible Man*.'

'Well, no but—'

She grabs my hand and drags me towards the gate. 'Come on, we've got what we wanted. Let's get out of here.'

# 10

Mum is wiping down the walls with a damp cloth. The whole room stinks of bleach.

'Where have you been?' she says. 'And why haven't you been answering your phones?'

'We missed two buses, *didn't* we, Archie?'

Maybe I'm getting better at lying. 'Yes, sorry, Mum. It won't happen again.'

'I got you fish and chips,' she says. 'But I'll have to warm them up in the microwave.'

'Great, thanks, Mum.'

'They don't cook the chips in the same oil as the fish, do they?'

'No, Izzy. I checked.' (Maybe Mum's getting better at lying too.)

And I'm two bites into my battered sausage when the shouting starts again; different voices from last night, but just as angry.

'Well, that's great,' says Izzy. 'How am I going to get my homework done?'

Izzy's pretty angry too. She only posted them

ten minutes ago, but she's already furious that no one has commented on the photos of our 'new house' – apart from Clint, of course, which only seemed to make things worse.

'I'm sorry, my love,' says Mum, sinking onto the bed with an exhausted groan. 'We'll have to get you some earplugs.'

'There's no table to write on anyway,' says Izzy. 'So what's the point?'

'I wish I knew, Izzy. I wish I…'

'What's the matter, Mum?' I say, already frightened of what her answer might be.

'You don't want to know, Archie.'

'Yes, I do.'

'Yes, come on,' says Izzy. 'It can't be any worse than it already is.'

Mum dries her eyes and reaches half-heartedly for one of my chips. 'It's probably nothing to worry about. But before you got back, I had a quick look in the basement. There's a couple of washing machines and a dryer down there.'

Izzy is checking her phone again. By the look on her face, no one important in Year Ten has commented on her photos. 'What's that got to do with anything?'

'I was talking to a woman called Maxine. And she said that that … she said that…' Mum's a nurse. She's *supposed* to be good at breaking bad news. 'Maxine said they'd been living here for over eight months.'

'You have *got* to be joking,' says Izzy. 'Have you seen that disgusting plughole in the bathroom?'

'Never mind that,' I say. 'I told Dinger we'd only be here for six weeks.'

'That's what it says on the council website,' says Mum. 'But I'm not sure if—'

'Typical,' says Izzy. 'Why couldn't you just be straight with us for once?'

'Now you listen to me, young lady. I won't have you—'

'Stop it, stop it,' I say, scratching the top of my arm like crazy. 'You're only making it worse.'

They both stop shouting to watch me scratch.

'What's wrong with your arm, Archie?' says Mum. 'Take your sweatshirt off and let me have a look.'

'Earrggghh,' says Izzy, when she sees the lines of angry scabs running towards my ears. 'What are they?'

'Bed bug bites,' says Mum. 'Don't worry. I'll get

some cream tomorrow. Soap and water will be fine for now.'

'That's disgusting,' says Izzy. 'What are you going to do about it?'

Mum springs into action like the trained professional that she is, stripping both beds in under two minutes and examining the mattresses for signs of alien life. 'They don't look too bad to me,' she says, stuffing the sheets into a black bin liner and slinging it over her shoulder. 'I'll take this lot downstairs and put them in the washing machine.'

'And what are *we* going to do?' says Izzy.

'I thought you said you had some homework. You'd better get on with it, hadn't you?'

Izzy lays out her books on the brown carpet tiles and pretends to be reading. I curl up in the moulting armchair and try to convince myself that *Jade's Inspirational Jewellery* is just as good a subject for a TV show as embarrassing illnesses or blind dates.

Every few minutes Izzy reaches hopefully for

her vibrating phone. And every time she checks it, she looks a little bit sadder.

'What's the matter?' I say, trying not to sound too sarcastic. 'Don't they like our "new house"?'

'How should I know? No one's even noticed. Apart from you know who.'

'So what's the problem then?'

She pulls a half-eaten packet of biscuits from her rucksack. According to Izzy they're vegan friendly, but it's never a good sign when the Bourbons come out. 'It's Clint,' she says. 'Why can't he just leave me alone?'

'Because he likes you, of course.'

'Yes, yes, he does, doesn't he?' says Izzy, her chocolaty lips definitely turning upwards for a moment.

It doesn't seem like rocket science to me; it doesn't even seem like dividing fractions. 'You should call him, Wizz. Go on, you know you want to.'

Her hand hovers over her phone for a moment. 'I can't,' she says, reaching for another biscuit instead. 'He mustn't see me here. It would be the end of everything. I mean, look at it. What if we have to stay in this place forever?'

'But Mum said—'

'What does she know? Face it, Arch we *have* to keep it a secret.'

Caitlin has already stopped texting me about our 'rubbish internet' and Amir didn't even question my unlikely weekend visit to Nottingham. Maybe it's going to be easier than I thought.

'Spose so. But Clint's never going to give up, you know. He'll see right through your invisible new boyfriend.'

We sit in silence for the next few minutes while Jade gets all excited about her limited offer jewellery-making kit and Izzy's thumbs go into overdrive.

'There you go,' she says, handing me her phone. 'What do you think of *him*?'

It's a photo of a stubbly twenty-year-old with ripped jeans, slicked back hair and an earring. He looks like an idiot, but she's in a bad enough mood already, so I'm not going to tell Izzy that. 'He looks OK. Why?'

'Tomorrow morning in IT, I'm going to Photoshop him into all my profile pictures.'

'Who is he, anyway?'

'It's Hamish, Hamish ... Willcock,' she says,

reaching for another biscuit. 'He's my new boyfriend.'

Mum must have taken one of her sleeping pills. She's tossing and turning and saying weird things in her sleep. 'No, Dinger, you can't go roller-skating. What about all the fish?'

I've tried counting Premier League footballers. That sometimes works. But the alarm clock says five past midnight and I'm still wide awake. There are too many questions and not enough answers running riot in my head: How long are we going to be here? Does Mrs Watts know that Dinger hates having his ears touched? Why did the old man at Izzy's dream house look straight through me? What kind of an imaginary boyfriend has a name like Hamish Willcock?

Room 102 is doing my head in. It feels like the walls are closing in on me, and Izzy's snoring is like the icing on the birthday cake that I'm probably never going to get. This must be how it was for Tolstoy and Rasputin. They said at the pet shop that Russian Dwarf Hamsters were happy to share a cage. But no wonder Tolstoy … did what he did.

Maybe a quick walk would clear my head. If I don't get out of here, I'm scared I might do something stupid – like tell Izzy she snores, for instance. So even though I'm scared silly of what I might find, I tiptoe to the door and set off down the corridor in my bare feet.

There's not much to see: just an endless row of closed doors. I have no idea what's behind them, but every now and then I get a little clue: a baby crying, a late-night action movie, people shouting at each other in a language I don't understand and the sound of breaking glass.

The only way is down: three flights of smelly stairs and then another one to the basement. If this was one of those scary movies that Izzy likes, I'd be screaming at myself not to do it. But at least it's quieter down here; cooler too. And for some reason that I don't completely understand, I can't resist the green door at the end marked 'Laundry Room'.

The lights are on and it smells nice. Not scary at all; just three washing machines, a massive tumble dryer and a few plastic chairs. And I'm almost starting to feel better when a voice that I've never heard before gives me the fright of my life.

'I don't believe it. It's Archie Ebbs!'

# 11

'Who's there?' I say, turning clumsy circles like a rubbish celebrity in *Strictly*.

The owner of the voice sounds surprised. 'Wait a minute. You can hear me, can't you, Archie?'

What a weird question. 'Yes … of course. Where are you?'

'I'm over here,' says the voice.

'Well, *I* can't see … oh.'

Her white onesie must have blended in with the walls. A girl about my age, but a tiny bit taller, is sitting in front of the tumble dryer with a book in her hands.

'Sorry, I didn't see you there.'

'What you mean you can *see* me too?' she says. 'That's … awesome.'

All I want to do right now is get out of here. But I don't want her to think I'm scared. 'So … you … live here too, do you?'

'Why else would I be down in the Laundry Room at midnight?'

I wrack my brains for something clever to say. 'You might be a plumber or something.' (It sounded a lot better in my head.)

'That's right, Archie. And how many ten-year-old plumbers do you know?'

'OK. So what *are* you doing here?'

'I sneak down to the basement every night to read,' she says, waving her paperback at me. 'Most nights I just can't sleep. My sister, Elka, has terrible nightmares. And it's so hot up there'

'Tell me about it. *My* sister's nose is, like, two centimetres away from my pillow. And she snores like an angry warthog in a thunderstorm.'

'Gross!'

That's when I notice she's reading my favourite book (*Goodnight, Mr Tom*). Even Caitlin liked it, and she thinks reading is only for people who are rubbish at football.

'Brilliant, isn't it? I love the bit where Willie throws up at the end of his birthday party. Our teacher read it to us last year.'

And now she's laughing at me. 'Yes, I know that, Archie. I was there.'

'I'm pretty sure you weren't,' I say, already fed up with her know-it-all act. 'So how did you find out my name?'

'Are you trying to be funny?' she says, without the tiniest hint of a smile. 'I thought you'd stopped being funny, Archie.'

'Were you in Beavers or something?'

'You really don't remember me, do you?'

I study her carefully for clues. There's nothing particularly memorable about her: short dark hair, regular nose and a mouth full of … teeth – that kind of thing. No wait. She smells like green apples. 'Sorry, I don't think I do.'

'I'm Zofia,' she says.

'Who?'

'You know, Zofia – from school.'

'Oh … yeah … right,' I say, trying to sound like she's just revealed the murderer and suddenly everything makes sense – except it doesn't, of course. 'Were you the one at the school concert who…?'

'We've been in the same class for the last two years, Archie.'

'Have we?'

The girl in the white onesie nods impatiently. 'Look, I know you haven't been yourself lately. And you might not have seen me for a while. But I thought you'd at least remember my name.'

And then it clicks. Well, not clicks exactly. It's more like looking at a distant galaxy through the wrong end of a telescope. 'Wait … Zofia, right? I think I do remember you now. You're the girl with the funny name.'

Zofia nods, but she certainly doesn't smile.

'Of *course*,' I say, half remembering Josh's hilarious impersonation of her. 'But hang on a minute. You can't speak English, can you?'

'That was two years ago, Archie. I'm not stupid, you know.'

I'm only trying to make conversation. Why's she having a go at me?

'No, course not, Zofia. Your English is really good now.'

'Yes, and I don't know why I bothered. Hardly anyone ever talked to me anyway. And that was *before*.'

Maybe her English isn't as good as she thinks. I have no idea what she's on about. 'What's the matter? Don't you like school or something?'

She looks at me like I'm completely stupid. 'What do *you* think? From the first moment I got there all everyone did was laugh at my name.'

'And it's not even *that* funny.'

She makes a weird angry sound in the back of her throat and aims her book at the tumble dryer. '*You* were the one who started it, Archie. And you didn't even pronounce my name properly. It's Zofia Kieslowski.'

'I didn't mean to upset you,' I say, suddenly remembering how her whole body had turned bright red. 'I just like making people laugh.'

'You don't have to be funny the whole time to make people like you, Archie.'

'I said I'm sorry, didn't I?'

She bends down to pick up her book, brushing it off and holding it close, like a friendly cat. 'Forget it,' she whispers. 'It doesn't matter now anyway.'

I never really stopped being 'Anxious Archie' until I discovered the awesome power of jokes. They were my way of fitting in. But I never wanted to make people unhappy.

'Mind if I sit down, Zofia?'

''Spose so. As long as you don't say anything stupid.'

I leave a chair between us, just in case. 'What did you mean just now when you said that I'd stopped being funny?'

'Sorry. I wasn't trying to be mean or anything, Archie. But I've noticed how unhappy you've been.'

Just because she's right, doesn't mean I'm going to admit it.

'No, I haven't. Why would you say that?'

'It doesn't matter. Let's talk about something else.'

'No, let's not,' I say, wishing I had some books to throw. 'I demand to know why you think I'm unhappy.'

Zofia shrugs. 'Well, you don't talk to your friends anymore. You always look really tired. And you've stopped telling those rubbish jokes.'

'No, I haven't,' I say, not even bothering to correct the 'rubbish' part. 'I told that one about the world's worse thesaurus.' (*Not only is it terrible, it's terrible.*)

'Yes, and no one laughed, did they?'

'Well I...' And now she's *really* getting on my nerves. 'How would *you* know? Have you been spying on me or something?'

'I've told you, Archie. I'm on the table right behind you. We're in the same class.'

'Oh yeah,' I say, turning angrily to face her. 'So how come I've never seen you?'

She stares down at her fluffy bunny slippers. 'You wouldn't believe me anyway.'

'I might,' I say, suddenly realising I've hardly thought about all my other problems for at least two minutes. 'Try me.'

Zofia takes a deep breath. 'The reason you haven't seen me is because ... sometime last year I turned invisible.'

Did she say what I just thought she just said?

'Eh?'

'I said, the reason you haven't seen me, Archie, is because just before Christmas, I completely disappeared.'

I laugh politely, but I'm starting to feel pretty uncomfortable.

'Yeah, very funny, Zofia. I thought I was the one who told rubbish jokes.'

'And I thought you might understand,' she says, pressing her book to her forehead so I can't see her face. 'It all started when Dad lost his job and we got evicted from our flat. No one took much notice of me at school anyway, but at least I'd made a couple of friends. A few weeks after we moved into this place, I realised that no one could see me anymore.'

'Wait a minute,' I say, suddenly remembering something we did in literacy. 'This is that thing Mr Blott was talking about, isn't it? It's a whatdoyoucallit, right, a … metaphor?'

Zofia slowly shakes her head. 'It's not a metaphor, Archie. The only people who can see me are my family. To everyone else I am *literally* invisible.'

'What do you mean?'

'What do you think I mean? They can't see me and they can't hear me either. It's like, I'm not even there.'

'What about your clothes?' I say, not quite sure why I'm even bothering to ask. 'If you were invisible, surely you'd look like a school uniform with no head.'

'This isn't some silly sci-fi movie, Archie. Obviously, my clothes are invisible too.'

This is probably going to sound stupid. But it's actually the first thought that came into my head. 'Don't be silly, Zofia. If you were completely invisible, why would you bother turning up for school?'

She comes out from behind her book. Her eyes are red and puffy. 'Where else could I go? I can't stay here all day. At least I feel safe at school. And so long as I self-register every morning, no one even notices I'm not there.'

I ought to tell her she's crazy. But she looks so sad. 'OK then, answer me this. If you're invisible, how come *I* can see you now?'

She thinks for a long time, gently tapping the floor with fluffy bunny slippers. 'Yes, that is weird, isn't it? Maybe it's because all your friends have started to ignore you.'

'No, they haven't.'

'If you say so, Archie.'

It's true they don't text me anymore. And they never include me in their Awesomeopolis planning. But it's kind of my fault in a way. Keeping Manton House a secret is so much easier when we're not really talking.

'And what's that got to do with it anyway?'

Zofia shrugs. 'I don't know. Maybe you need some new friends.'

By now I'm so furious I just want to get away from her. 'Well, I don't, all right? And as for all that invisible stuff. You might think it's funny. But it's not.'

'Whatever,' says Zofia, opening her book

again. 'Maybe you're not ready yet. But I'm down here most nights, Archie. I'll see you around.'

'I doubt it,' I say, stumbling angrily to the door. 'We're only here for six weeks.'

Zofia obviously finds this very funny. 'OK, fine. I'll see you at school tomorrow.'

'Not if I see you first.'

# 12

Want to know why I look so fed up? It's because I'm trying to hide from Zofia. Two weeks ago I hardly knew who she was, but ever since our meeting in the Laundry Room she's been following me round the school like a super-annoying imaginary friend.

No wonder no one ever talks to her. Wherever I turn, there she is, ready and waiting with a silly comment. Like when I don't get an invitation to Josh's birthday outing to Wembley Stadium.

*Don't worry about it, Archie. It sounds dead boring if you ask me.*

Or the time I tell Amir I can't film the final scene of *The Revenge of the Fruit* (Episode Eight: *Attack of the Courgettes)* because of 'an important dental appointment' and he doesn't even try to rearrange it.

*It's not because you're a bad actor, Archie. And who wants to be an evil artichoke anyway?*

But no matter how many times I beg her to leave me alone, she just won't listen. She even pats me on the back when the team for the District Sports goes up and my name isn't on it.

*It's just not fair, Archie. Everyone knows you're the best runner.*

That's why I'm in the library at lunchtime, curled up on a beanbag in Mrs Goodall's 'Chillout Area' beneath a giant copy of *Where's Wally?*. No one seems to bother me here. Caitlin's stopped asking me why I don't play football on the field anymore and even the Harry Potter kids who hang out here every day have stopped trying to include me in their important debates: *Is Snape a villain? Who would you rather sit next to: Cho Chang or Neville Longbottom?*

And I'm right in the middle of a really lovely dream (Dinger is lying across my knees telling me about his top six favourite cat treats and I'm asking him how he learned to talk), when a distant voice drags me back to reality.

'Hello, Archie. I'm glad I've caught you. Mind if I have a quick word?'

At first I think it's Zofia. 'Look, stop following me around. You're so annoying. You know that, don't you?'

But the voice sounds a bit deeper. 'It won't take

long, Archie, I promise. A couple of minutes, that's all.'

I yawn and try to force my eyes open. 'Oh, it's you … sorry.'

Mr Blott is standing over me with a steaming mug of tea in one hand and a concerned look on his face. 'Who did you think it was?'

'Oh, no one, just … I must have been dreaming.'

Mr Blott pulls up another beanbag. 'You've not really been yourself lately, have you, Archie?'

'Haven't I?'

He shakes his head. 'I hope you don't mind me asking, but is everything all right at home?'

Home – if you can call it that – is horrible. What's worse, it looks like we're going to be living in Manton House forever. When we first moved there, Mum spent the whole time on the phone to the council or writing emails to our local MP. But just lately she seems to have given up. And Izzy is doing her best to make *my* life as miserable as hers, especially after her romantic trip to London with Hamish Willcock that not a single person in Year Ten commented on. No wonder all I want to do is sleep.

'Home's great,' I say, trying to force a smile. 'Couldn't be better.'

Mr Blott looks like he's forcing a smile too. 'I've tried contacting your mum a couple of times on parentmail, but she hasn't got back to me.'

'She's really busy at work,' I say, wishing he'd just leave me alone. 'What did you want her for anyway?'

He takes a sip of tea and stares thoughtfully at the Year Five recycling displays. 'I'm a little bit concerned about your schoolwork, Archie. Nothing to worry about, but you always look so tired. And you don't seem to participate in lessons anymore.'

It's true. I'm so exhausted that every time he asks a question my brain freezes, so I've stopped putting my hand up. Luckily my lying skills have improved a lot lately. 'It's … er, Izzy. She's got a trombone exam coming up and I haven't been getting much sleep.'

'Oh … well … that explains it then,' he says, scrambling to his feet. 'Izzy loves her music, doesn't she?'

'Oh yes.'

He starts to leave, but then turns back. 'You would tell me, wouldn't you, Archie?'

'Tell you what?'

'If anything was wrong. Don't keep it bottled up inside. If there's something you want to talk about, just give me a shout.'

Like I said, I'm really getting the hang of this lying thing. 'Yeah, definitely. Is that all, Mr Blott?'

He flashes his super-white teeth at me. 'There was something else actually. I've had rather a brilliant idea. And I have a feeling you could help me with it.'

All I really want to do is go back to sleep. 'What kind of an idea?'

'I know it's a few weeks off yet, Archie. But I'd like you to be my compere for the talent show at the Leavers' Party. All you'd have to do is introduce the acts and tell a few jokes.'

Mr Blott's school talent shows are legendary. Last year he got Mrs Goodall and the dinner ladies to dress up as Little Mix. And, just for a second, I'm actually quite tempted.

'I don't think so, thanks.'

'Why not? You were the first person I thought of.'

It's hard to explain. There was a time when I loved being the centre of attention. These days I just want to fade into the background. 'I'm sorry. I don't think I can. Why don't you ask Josh?'

'Right… Yes, I'll … leave you to it then,' says Mr Blott, his sunny smile turning into something more thoughtful. 'The trombone is a lovely instrument. But you *can* have too much of a good thing. Perhaps you should try some ear plugs.'

Thank goodness he's gone. There are still twenty minutes until the next lesson. So I grab *Where's Wally?* and disappear back into the beanbag. Maybe at last I can catch up on some sleep.

But I've only just closed my eyes when the smell of green apples shocks me awake again.

'Well, that was nice of him, wasn't it?' says Zofia.

'Where did *you* come from?'

'I've been here the whole time,' she says, grabbing *Where's Wally?* and sitting down beside me. 'You look so unhappy, Archie. I'm worried about you.'

'Well, don't be,' I say. 'What do you want anyway?

'We've got a lot in common, haven't we?' says Zofia, running her finger across the page until it lands on the man in the red bobble hat. 'We even live in the same building. I just thought it would be nice if we could be friends.'

'I don't need any more friends,' I say, feeling a bit dizzy after I jump to my feet. 'Especially not a weird girl like you. I've got loads of them already.'

She stands slowly and looks me straight in the eyes. 'So how come Josh, Caitlin and Amir are going to the beach without you?'

Maybe it's *my* fault. I've been so tired lately that I've not really had time for my friends. So after school when I hear Josh and Caitlin laughing like machine guns as they charge down the corridor towards the playground, I decide it's time to make an effort.

'Wait up, guys,' I say, trying hard to keep pace with them. 'What's so funny?'

'You probably wouldn't get it,' says Caitlin, taking out her tennis ball and flicking it to Josh as we emerge into the hot sunshine.

'Try me,' I say.

'You weren't there,' says Josh. 'It'll take too long to explain.'

'Oh, come on,' I say, putting in a pretty good tackle and grabbing the tennis ball. 'It sounds really funny.'

Caitlin isn't laughing anymore. 'Can I have my ball back please?'

'Only if you tell me what you were laughing about.'

Josh rolls his eyes at me. 'You had to be there, OK?'

'Had to be where?' I say.

'You'd better tell him,' says Caitlin. 'Or he'll never shut up.'

'OK,' says Josh. 'So, we found this carrot at Amir's sleepover and it looked just like a...' He looks at Caitlin and they both burst out laughing. 'You know, a "thingy"?'

Maybe it's because my mum's a nurse. But it doesn't actually sound that funny. 'Oh ... right. So where are you off to then, guys?'

'We're going down the beach with Amir,' says Caitlin.

And I'm half hoping for an invitation. Until they walk straight past me, like I'm not even there.

But believe it or not, I'm not the most

miserable-looking person in the playground. That award goes to the person who's waiting for me by the recycling bin. In fact, if I was *actually* invisible, it would probably be quite useful right now. But he spots me straight away.

'Oi, Arch, over here!'

I try to pretend I haven't seen him, but he follows me across the playground like a depressed bloodhound. 'Slow down, Arch. I need to talk to you.'

Talking to my sister's 'ex' is strictly forbidden, but Clint's like family. How can I possibly ignore him? 'Hi Clint, how's it going?'

His eyes are red and he looks like he hasn't combed his hair for weeks. (Come to think of it, his hair always looks like that.) He reaches into his 'Clint Hearts Izzy' rucksack and pulls out a Capri Sun. 'I got you this.'

I've really missed him. Not to mention his vegan spaghetti bolognese. 'Thanks.'

'How is she?'

'Who?' I say, pretending I don't know what he's talking about.

'Izzy, of course.'

I pick up the pace, but he stumbles after me.

'She should be here soon. Why don't you ask her yourself?'

'She went home as soon as she saw me,' he says, waving his violin case at the bus stop. 'Why won't she talk to me, Arch? What did I do wrong?'

'I'm sorry, I can't—'

'She is all right, isn't she? Tell me, Archie. I just want to know she's OK.'

Izzy isn't OK. In fact she couldn't be less OK if she tried. I think she hates the B&B more than I do. There's nowhere to do her homework and every time she tries to practise her trombone, someone starts banging on the wall. But it's worse than that. She can't even be bothered to scream at Mum anymore – most of the time she just sits on the bed staring at her phone.

'She's fine,' I say, relieved that at least my new-found lying skills haven't deserted me. 'She's just had a lot on her mind lately.'

Clint looks heartbroken. 'So what's he like then?'

'Who?'

'Hamish.'

'*Who*?'

'You know. Hamish Willcock. Her new...' He can hardly bear to say it. '...boyfriend.'

I turn back towards main reception. 'Oh, *that* Hamish. He's … OK, I suppose.'

'He's not right for her,' says Clint, following me up to the door. 'His hair's all wrong and he doesn't even like spaghetti.'

I have to get away from him. I can't stand seeing him like this. 'Sorry, Clint, I've forgotten my homework diary. I'll have to go back in and get it.'

'Please, Arch. Just tell me where you live. She won't talk to me at school.'

'Look, you can't come in,' I said, pushing open the door. 'You have to get a lanyard and everything.'

Clint nods. 'All right, I'll wait. I'll wait forever if that's what it takes.'

The bus will be here in a few minutes. I *have* to think of something. If Clint keeps flashing his hound-dog eyes at me I'm sure to tell him everything. And Izzy will never forgive me. 'OK. See you in a bit then. Won't be long.'

But instead of going out through main reception, I creep down the corridor to the boys' toilets. Luckily Mr Messy the caretaker is so busy rounding up recycling that he doesn't see me slip inside.

Callum Critchlow once boasted that he'd climbed out of the toilet window to escape from a teaching assistant. And, just for once, he was obviously telling the truth. I grab hold of the paper dispenser and climb onto the sink. The window is just wide enough for me to squeeze through and jump down into the playground.

Clint is still waiting outside main reception. If I'm careful, he'll never notice me.

But I'm only as far as the netball court when I realise my bus is coming up the hill. I know it's risky, but I don't have any choice. All I can do is make a run for it.

I race across the playground and out into the street, not daring to look back. The bus is getting closer. So I stick out my arm and try to wave it down as I run across the road towards the bus stop.

And just as I'm congratulating myself on successfully avoiding Clint, I catch my foot in a pothole and fly up into the air. 'Yeaaaahhhhhhh.' Splat.

I'm so stunned I can hardly move. All I can do is wave my arms and shout, 'Stop, stop.'

But the bus just keeps on coming.

'Stop, stop!'

The bus is so close I can taste the petrol fumes.

'Stop, stop. Why don't you—?'

I close my eyes and prepare for the worst. The next thing I know, two hands grab hold of my arm and drag me from the gutter.

The brakes screech as the number 27 skids to a halt.

The driver jumps out and rushes across to us. The sweat is dripping off him as he helps me to my feet. 'Where the hell did you spring from?'

'I kept waving at you, but you wouldn't stop.'

'It's not *his* fault,' says Zofia, brushing dust off the back of my shirt. 'He obviously couldn't see you. Lucky I was around to save your life!'

The bus driver hitches up his trousers and shakes his head. 'I'm sorry, son. I didn't see you until the last minute. You're not a cat by any chance?'

'What are you…?'

'Talk about nine lives,' says the bus driver. 'How did you manage to jump out of the way like that?'

'It was me, stupid,' says Zofia, flexing her arm muscles at him. 'That is so funny, isn't it, Archie?'

But the bus driver is obviously so shaken up that he doesn't take any notice of her. And once he's satisfied that I'm definitely OK, he climbs back into his cab.

Zofia is staring thoughtfully at the number plate. 'I think I might know why you can see me, Archie.'

'Not this again, why?'

'It's obvious, isn't it,' says Zofia, running up the steps without even flashing her bus pass. 'It's because you're starting to turn invisible too.'

'Stop it, Zofia. It wasn't even funny the first time.'

'Come on, Archie, you'll miss the bus.'

'I'm not coming,' I say, suddenly realising what I've got to do. 'There's someone I need to see first.'

'Well, be careful,' calls Zofia. 'You can't just walk into the road anymore. Turning invisible is a health-and-safety nightmare!'

# 13

I feel sick when I see the For Sale sign outside our old house. The flowers in Mum's hanging basket are dead and my bedroom window looks all wrong without the yellow curtains.

And I might as well be invisible because I feel like a ghost, come back to the haunt the one place where I was really happy. Perhaps that's why I'm tempted to sneak down to the back garden and check out the hamsters' graveyard. But that's not why I'm here.

'Dinger! Diiiiinger! Where are you, boy? Come on, Dinger. It's me, Archie!'

Yes, I know. Cats don't come when they're called. Not unless you're carrying a tin of Whiskas. That's what I love about Dinger. You can never make him do anything he doesn't want to – which is probably why I couldn't teach him to read in Year One.

But I really need to make sure he's OK. So I suppose there's only one thing for it. I cross the road to Mrs Watts' house (it's the one with the NO JUNK MAIL OR COLD CALLERS sign), straighten my school sweatshirt and ring the bell.

The door opens and a grey face appears. 'Who's there?'

'It's me Mrs Watts, Archie.'

'I can't see you,' she says, her grey eyes seeming to look straight through me. 'I hope you're not selling something.'

A shiver of panic fizzes up my spine. 'What do you mean you can't see me? I'm Archie Ebbs. You must remember. I used to put your bins out.'

Mrs Watts' laugh sounds like a sheep with a bad cold. 'Silly me,' she says, reaching for the pair of glasses hanging round her neck and peering at me through her inch-thick lenses. 'That's better. Now, what can I do for you, Archie?'

'Well, I was just … passing and I wondered if I could pop in and see Dinger?'

'Does your mother know that you're here?'

'Oh yes,' I say, staring guiltily at the welcome mat. 'It was her idea.'

Mrs Watts doesn't sound very convinced. 'Well, it's rather inconvenient. But I suppose you'd better come in.'

The house smells of buttered toast and cats. Mrs Watts leads me towards the booming television in the lounge. Bimbo and Mrs Thatcher are sprawled across the furniture, like furry emperors, but I can't see Dinger anywhere.

'Is he all right?' I say, checking behind the sofa. 'Did you remember what I told you about not liking having his ears touched?'

'Schrödinger is as fit as a fiddle,' says Mrs Watts, using the full name that Mum gave him, but neither Izzy nor me could pronounce. 'Now sit down, Archie. And I'll bring you a nice glass of orange squash.'

Mrs Watts disappears to the kitchen. I sink into the leather armchair and stare suspiciously at Bimbo and Margaret Thatcher. I've never liked the look of Bimbo. And Margaret Thatcher has a big scar above one eye because she's always fighting. How could Dinger possibly be happy in a place like this?

'Dinger? Dinger?' I say, reaching for Mrs Watts' remote and turning down *Escape to the Country*. 'Where are you, boy? There's something I want to tell you.'

That's another good thing about Dinger; he's a

great listener and he can always keep a secret – which is lucky, because he knows more about me than anyone in the world. Apart from Mum, of course.

So where is he? I could really use a cuddle right now. Plus, I want to tell him about nearly being run over by a bus. But it looks like this whole journey has been a complete waste of time. How will I know he's OK if I haven't actually seen him?

But just as I'm starting to give up hope – and the couple on the television are falling 'head over heels in love' with an eight-bedroom converted barn in the Cotswolds – I hear a familiar voice:

'Miaoooooow.'

'Dinger! Where are you boy? I can't see you.'

A moment later, a small ginger face peeps out from behind the piano.

And with a whoop of happiness, I race across the purple rug and scoop him into my arms. 'Oh Dinger, I've missed you *so* much. Have you missed me?' I bury my nose in the back of his head and whisper into his raggedy ears. 'Don't worry, Dinger, it won't be for much longer. I'll get you out of here, I promise. You are all right, aren't you, boy? Is old Mrs Watts looking after you?'

'Of course I am,' says Mrs Watts, who's standing right behind me with a plastic beaker in her hand. 'Now sit down, Archie. And I'll give you your juice.'

The next ten minutes are the happiest ten minutes of my life for months. Dinger sounds happy too. His purrs are so loud you could probably hear them in outer space. And I don't even have to say anything because, apart from the fact that Mrs Watts is watching her programme, I'm pretty sure Dinger can read my mind anyway.

'I'm sorry, Archie,' says Mrs Watts. 'But I'm afraid you'll have to go now. *The Chase* is on in ten minutes. And I want to make myself a ham sandwich.'

'Can I just say goodbye to Dinger first?'

Mrs Watts nods impatiently. 'Yes, of course. But please hurry up, dear. I don't want to miss anything.'

I hate it when Mum kisses me in public so Dinger probably hates it too, but I can't help myself. 'Bye Dinger,' I say, kissing him softly on both his front paws and trying not to get tears on his fur. 'I love you, boy. And I wish you could live with us in Manton House. But I'm always thinking about you. And I promise I'll come back and see you again soon.'

Mrs Watts hurries me to the door and unfastens the safety chain. 'Goodbye, Archie. It was very nice to see you. Please send my regards to your mother.'

'I will, Mrs Watts.'

She opens the door and practically pushes me out. 'Oh and Archie, there's just one more thing.'

'Yes, Mrs Watts?'

'I think it's for the best if you don't come here again. I shall telephone your mother to explain properly. But it's very confusing for Schrödinger. And I don't want to interrupt his new routine.'

# 14

It's the last lesson on Monday afternoon and I'm feeling pretty tired and miserable. Mum says I mustn't go anywhere near Mrs Watts' house ('Don't forget she's doing us a big favour, Archie') so I've been lying awake all night worrying about Dinger. I'm pretty sure he's losing weight. Maybe Bimbo and Mrs Thatcher have been stealing his food.

And to make matters worse, I just told a really good joke and not a single person in the class, not even Zofia, laughed at it: *I hate my job as an origami teacher. There's so much paperwork!*

On the plus side, Callum Critchlow has been banished to Mrs Goodall's office since lunchtime. Giving a Year Five a wedgie didn't seem like a piece of a comic genius to me. But it still got a bigger laugh than my joke. At least with the noisiest kid in the class out of the way, I can rest my head on my desk until the bell goes. Who knows, I might even be able to get some sleep?

'OK, guys,' says Mr Blott. 'Do you want the good news or do you want the good news?'

'The good news!'

He takes his book safe from the bottom of the pile on his desk and waves it at us. It was a present from one of his old classes and it's actually pretty cool. It *looks* like a book (*Les Miserables* is his favourite musical) but inside is a money box with a special code and everything.

Mr Blott opens the front cover and pulls out a handful of bank notes. 'Well, I've been counting your Leavers' party money. And it looks like we're over halfway there.'

Everyone cheers. Apart from yours truly, who abandons all hope of a sneaky nap.

'So, well done those of you who've already contributed. Chelsey, your mud cake was amazing; so was Ryan and Shelley's sponsored silence. But don't forget, there's still plenty of time to think of some great fundraising ideas.'

Josh puts his hand up. 'Me, Amir and Caitlin are going to sell our slime.'

'Well, there you go then,' says Mr Blott. 'Looks like we're going to get our inflatable assault course, guys.'

Five hours later, after the cheering finally dies down, Mr Blott introduces our latest star of the week. 'Righty ho then. Let's have a big hand for Amir, shall we?'

And there's yet more cheering as Amir makes his way to the front of the class and puts his memory stick in the laptop.

'So Amir,' says Mr Blott. 'What have you got for us?'

'This afternoon I'm going to talk about Top Table Productions and *The Revenge of the Fruit* movies.'

At least it's something interesting for a change. Maybe my terrible day is getting better at last.

'Fabulous,' says Mr Blott. 'We were watching the one with the killer pineapple in the staff room just the other day. That was genius.'

The killer pineapple was *my* idea.

'I wrote my first movie script in Year Two,' says Amir. A photo of a six-year-old film director appeared on the white board. Most of us laugh, but a few of the girls go 'aaahhh'.

'It was called *The Little Bus Who Didn't Want to Be Late*.'

Amir's PowerPoint is quite funny until he

stops talking about his early influences (*Sean the Sheep* and the *Star Wars* movies) and moves on to the formation of Top Table Productions.

'Here's a short clip from *The Revenge of the Fruit,* Episode One: *The Tomatoes Strike Back.* I wrote the script. But like all our films it was a *collaborative* effort.' Collaboration is one of the 'school values'. He smiles at Mr Blott to make sure he realises that he's worked it into his speech deliberately.

Amir is going down a storm with the rest of the class. But the longer he goes on, the angrier I get. He talks forever about Josh's ability to blow up vegetables and what a good actor Caitlin is. So why has he hardly even mentioned *me*? Amir might have written all the scripts, but some of the best jokes (the dancing cabbages, the dream sequence in *The Grapefruit Awakens)* were mine. I'm not in any of the clips either. The best he can manage is the back of my head in the fight between Garth Vader and the grapes.

'Filming is definitely the funnest part. And I really like editing too. But the bit I enjoy most is where we all get together and watch it for the first time. Josh says that...'

How could he do that? He's practically edited me out of the whole story. I'm just as much a part of Top Table Productions as the rest of them. I even came up with the name. It's a long time since I've spoken in class, but I just can't stop myself.

'What about me?' I say.

Amir just goes on talking. '...and sometimes you can use music to make a joke funnier. I remember when we made *Grapefruit Awakens* Caitlin found something on Spotify that was...'

'I *said*, what about me?'

It's so rude. Amir just ignores me and carries on. '...and slow motion is good too. I used to edit in Windows Movie Maker, but now I prefer...'

By now I'm shouting at the top of my voice. 'What about me? What about me? WHAT ABOUT ME?'

Amir doesn't hesitate. It's like he hasn't even heard. '...and one day, I want to go to Hollywood and meet some of my heroes. That would be...'

And the rest of the class are just the same. They're so engrossed in Top Table Productions and *The Revenge of the Fruit* movies that not one of them turns my way.

'Mr Blott, Mr Blott,' I scream. 'He's not

listening to me. You've got to make him answer my question.'

Except Mr Blott isn't listening either. He's looking straight through me with a faraway smile on his face.

But then I remember what he told Callum Critchlow about always putting your hand up. 'Mr Blott, Mr Blott,' I shout, jumping to my feet and punching the air with my upraised arm. 'It's not fair. I was in those films too. And he hasn't even mentioned me. Look, see, I've got my hand up like you said. Why won't you...?'

And that's when I feel another hand on my shoulder. 'Calm down, Archie,' says Zofia. 'There's no point shouting, they can't hear you anymore. I *knew* there was a reason you could see me. It's because we're both invisible now. Look!' She runs across to Mr Blott and pretends to aim a punch at his face. He doesn't even flinch. 'See what I mean?'

'No!' I say, climbing onto the table and waving my arms. 'Stop it, stop it. This isn't funny anymore. Why are you doing this to me?'

But every eye in the class, including Mr Blott's is fixed firmly on Amir, who keeps on talking as if nothing has happened. '...And probably the best special effect we've ever done is the disappearing raspberry in *Phantom Lettuce*. That was when...'

Zofia offers me her hand. 'Get down, Archie. You might hurt yourself.

I grab hold of it and climb down from the table. 'What's happening?'

'I've told you,' says Zofia. 'You've turned invisible, Archie. Now do you believe me?'

'All right,' I say, taking back my hand. 'Now, please, just leave me alone for a bit.'

I have to get out of here. And Zofia doesn't try to stop me as I run to the door. Mrs Goodall doesn't even tell me off for running in the corridor as I fly past her on my way to the boys' toilets.

Somebody is in the cubicle already, so I pace between the door and the paper dispenser, staring at the floor. I knew something was wrong, but I can't believe that Zofia was right. And suddenly some of the other weird stuff that's been happening lately is starting to make sense: the bus driver who couldn't see me, the old man by the swimming pool. It must have been because I was turning invisible. I was waving my arms around and screaming my head off back there. And they just couldn't see me. But that's impossible, isn't it?

And suddenly I have this uncontrollable urge to puke.

Luckily, I'm in the right place and I just about make it to the wash basin as a shaft of rhubarb-flavoured vomit launches itself into orbit. I turn away in disgust and collapse sobbing onto the cold tiled floor.

'You all right, mate?' calls a familiar voice from the cubicle. 'Is Mrs Goodall looking for you too?'

Come to think of it, Callum Critchlow is hardly ever in class anymore. Maybe this is where he hangs out. 'I'm OK,' I call. 'I'm just looking for something.'

But he obviously can't hear me. 'I *said*, is she after you too?'

'Is who after me?'

'Don't talk much do you?' says Callum. 'Best to keep your mouth shut anyway. What year are you in? Not Year Five, are you? Do us a favour, eh.

Tell that Mason kid I didn't mean to hurt him. It was only a wedgie!'

'What's happening to me?' I whisper. 'How is this even possible?'

'You sure you're all right, mate?' says Callum. 'I thought I smelled puke.'

It's already the weirdest situation I've ever been in. But hearing Callum Critchlow being nice to someone is making it even weirder.

'Splash some water on your face and have a little drink. It'll make you feel better.'

And I've just clawed my way up the basin and sprinkled myself with cold water when there's a knock on the door and in walks Zofia. 'There you are, Archie. I was getting really worried about you.'

'You can't come in here. It's the boys' toilets. And Callum Critchlow's in there.'

Zofia smiles. 'Don't worry. He can't see us, can he?'

'I'm out of here,' says Callum, pushing open the cubicle door. 'My taxi will be coming soon. I'll see you la—' He looks round the 'empty' toilet and shakes his head. 'Well, that was rude. Where have they gone?'

Zofia turns off the tap.

'I just wanted to make sure you were OK, Archie. How are you feeling?'

'I've just found out I'm invisible. How do you think I feel?'

'I know,' says Zofia sympathetically. 'It's horrible. But you'll get used to it, I promise. Just like you'll get used to living in Manton House.'

'No, I won't,' I say, kicking open the toilet door and setting off down the corridor. 'How can I ever be happy if no one can see me?'

'Your family can still see you,' says Zofia, hurrying after me. 'And so can I, Archie.'

'I don't want to talk about it, OK?'

'Fine,' says Zofia, as the bell goes and a swarm of excited Year Fours make a dash for freedom. 'But there's something I want to tell you first.'

'Please, Zofia. All I want is to get out of here.'

'Well before you go, I just wanted to say … I just wanted to say…' She stares shyly at the floor. 'I've been so lonely, Archie. It would be really great to have a proper invisible friend.'

'I … *suppose*.'

'Disappearing is the worst thing that's ever happened to me,' says Zofia, pulling me out of the way of Mr Messy the caretaker who's about to run us down with his cleaning trolley. 'But maybe if we stick together, school could be, you know, a bit of a laugh. What do you, say, Archie? When we come back tomorrow, why don't we have some fun?'

But having fun is the last thing on my mind. 'Sorry, Zofia. I think I'd be better off on my own at the moment. I'll probably spend the day in the library, catching up on some sleep. See you later.'

'OK ... if that's what you want, Archie. But let me know if you change your mind.'

The playground is heaving with parents and childminders. But not one of them takes any notice of me as I shout 'get out my way' and wave my hand in their faces in a last desperate attempt to make myself visible again.

Izzy is waiting for me in the bus shelter. 'Why are you so early?' she says, returning immediately to her phone. 'You normally take, like, forever. What's the matter with you?'

At least *she* can still see me. Zofia said that would happen. But I'm so relieved all I want to do is give her a big hug. (This is Izzy we're talking about here, so obviously I don't.) 'You can see me!

You can see me! You can see me, can't you, Wizz? And you can hear me too.'

'Look if you're trying to be funny, Archie. I'm not in the mood.

'Sorry. I'm just pleased to see you, that's all.'

The bus is coming up the hill. Izzy sets off in the opposite direction. 'Shut up and follow me,' she says. 'There's somewhere I want to go.'

# 15

Instead of waiting at the bus stop outside the library, Izzy walks straight past it and runs up the steps.

'Where are you going?' I ask.

'Where do you think?'

'But why?' I say, following her through the revolving doors.

'Because I need somewhere quiet to do my homework for a change. That place is a nightmare. I can't concentrate and it stinks.'

'Does Mum know about this?'

'I told her this morning,' says Izzy. 'She thinks it's a great idea.'

'Well, no one told me. What am *I* supposed to do?'

Izzy is rooting around in her rucksack. She's tried to scrub it off, but the faint outline of 'Izzy and Clinton 4 ever' is clearly visible on the front pocket. 'Here's your library card. Why don't you go and mess about on the computers? I'll come and find you in about an hour.'

Izzy goes off to the reference library, leaving me to find my own way to the graveyard of old-fashioned computers behind the magazine section on the second floor. There's no one there; just one old man dozing by the newspapers. Lucky he can't see me or he'd probably try to start a conversation about the good old days or how mobile phones have ruined civilisation as we know it.

And then I spot his guide dog. That's quite ironic actually. Even if I wasn't invisible, he wouldn't be able see me. But I still select the cubicle furthest away from him and type in the number at the top of my library card. One of them smells weird, and I don't think it's the dog!

It's quite exciting to begin with. I haven't been online since we got evicted – except at school, but that doesn't count because all the best sites are blocked. So I go straight to YouTube because I know exactly what I want to watch first.

I haven't actually seen the latest *Revenge of the Fruit* movie, but I overheard Amir and Caitlin saying how brilliant it is. And although I never got round to filming my final scenes in *Attack of the Courgettes*, I'm really looking forward to the bit at the beginning where the Evil Artichoke drowns the grapes in the washing up bowl.

At first I think Amir must have changed the running order in the final edit. But after a few minutes I realise that every single shot of me as the Evil Artichoke has been cut. There's a new villain, the Malevolent Mushroom (Josh with his Mum's grey handbag over his head) and the scene with Donald Trump's wig has been replaced by a really lame montage of Josh, Amir and Caitlin eating vegetable kebabs.

I don't know whether to be angry or sad. I mean, it's not completely their fault, is it? Even before I turned invisible, I was doing my best to avoid them. Being friends at school is impossible now. But maybe, just maybe, we can still be friends online.

And I know exactly where to find them.

Paris and London are pretty good, but I've spent so many happy hours in Awesomeopolis that it's probably my favourite city in the word. The trouble is, it's just not the same anymore. I'd kind of promised myself that I'd never go back. And the moment I step into Joshamiraitlin Square I realise why. I feel like a stranger in my own city. There are more cars on the roads, the skyscrapers are higher, someone (probably Amir, he was always going on about it) has installed street lighting and they've replaced Buckingham Palace with a KFC.

**dark_matter**, **joshmaggedon** and ***caitmeister7*** are down by the harbour. I'm not sure what they're working on, but they've all gathered on a floating platform looking across at the city.

I really don't want to mess this up. Maybe they'll say something nice about me. So I crouch behind a crane and listen to their conversation for a bit. All they talk about is Amir's new haircut; what's better, Cheesestrings or Pepperami?; who does the best takeaway (I'm an expert on that); the dugouts at Wembley Stadium; Callum Critchlow's latest crimes against humanity; and some new shows on Netflix that I won't be able to watch. But not once do they mention me. Perhaps it's time to remind them who I am.

So I jump onto the platform and introduce myself:

**<archenemy>** *Hi guys. Wassup?*

But they're obviously too busy to take any notice.

**<joshmaggedon>** *You ready for this?*

<**dark_matter**> *Yeah. Let's do it!!!!!!!!!!!!!*

And that's when I see that they've built a long line of rocket launchers, each with its own missile.

< ***caitmeister7***> *I've set some time bombs. Let's nuke the whole thing.*

And suddenly, I feel like I'm going to be sick again.

<**joshmaggedon**> *Point the radar gun at the target and click on launch.*

*Who wants to go first?'*

I run round in circles and try to catch their attention.

<**archenemy**> *Guys NOOOOOO you can't do this. We all worked so hard on it.*

But **dark_matter** doesn't even hesitate.

The first missile crashes into the water. But it doesn't take them long to find their range and pretty soon they're taking it in turns to bombard the city.

*Yeoooooow,* says ***caitmeister7***, as she completely destroys the Olympic village.

*Woooowza* says **dark_matter** as the Empire State Building burst into flames.

**joshmaggedon** even climbs onto a lava missile and rides it straight into the Tower of London: *Geroooonimooo.*

*You died! (Respawn)*

**<dark_matter>** *Awesomeopolis was kids' stuff. We should have done this months ago.*

The whole city lies in ruins. Smoke is belching from the rooftops and vast craters have appeared in the shopping district.

**<dark_matter>** *Ha ha ha ha ha ha ha ha ha*

**<joshmaggedon>** *Wiiiiiiiiiicked!!!*

**< caitmeister7>** *lol!*

But I don't think it's funny at all. It was bad enough already, but this is without doubt the worst moment of my life so far.

Because I've just realised what it means. It's not only about the death of the city I love. The horrible truth has just blasted me in the face like a flamethrower. Not only am I invisible in real life, I'm invisible online too.

There is one good thing I suppose. At least no

one can witness the pathetic sight of my shoulders shaking uncontrollably, the deep sobs and my salty tears bombarding the keyboard.

'What's the matter, old son? You all right?

The old man and his guide dog must have wandered across from the newspapers.

'Please, just leave me alone,' I sniff. 'Wait a minute. How come you see me anyway?'

'I may be blind,' said the old man. 'But I know when a young fellow's upset.'

I still feel numb. And it doesn't make much sense. 'Oh … right … yeah.'

'You'd better have this,' he says, offering me his snotty handkerchief.

I quickly wipe my eyes on my sleeve. 'It's OK, thanks. I'll be fine in a minute.'

'What's the matter?' says the old man. 'Trouble at school, is it?'

Well, where would *you* start? The fall of Awesomeopolis, living in one room, turning invisible – or being chucked out of your own home? 'It's a bit more complicated than that.'

'It always is,' says the old man with a knowing nod. 'But you know what you should do, don't you?'

I don't have a clue. It's a million miles worse than a pizza and hot chocolate with marshmallows problem. 'Not really, no.'

The old man reaches down and ruffles his guide dog's neck. 'Now Towser here is a professional, of course. But that doesn't mean we can't be comrades. In fact, he's as good a listener as my dear old Beryl, God rest her.'

'What do you mean?'

'Simple, isn't it, Towser?' says the old man, taking a scarf from his Sainsbury's bag and wrapping it round his wrinkly neck. 'A problem shared is a problem halved. So if you want to feel better about something, your best bet is a good old chin wag with a friend.'

A moment later, I feel a slobbery tongue on my hand. It ought to make me feel better. But it only reminds me how terrible things are. 'That's one of the problems,' I sob. 'I haven't got any friends.'

# 16

Izzy has obviously been checking her phone again because she's spent the whole journey back to the B&B telling me what a 'total waste of space' I am. Perhaps the other passengers think she's on her phone, or she's one of those sad people who talk to themselves on buses. Or maybe it's happening to Izzy too, because no one takes much notice of the angry girl with the trombone case shouting at the empty seat next to her.

'It's all your fault, you little worm. If you'd taken some decent photos like I asked, my friends wouldn't be treating me like this. Even Clint has stopped texting.'

'I thought that's what you wanted.'

'Don't be an idiot,' says Izzy, her nostrils flaring, like the barrel of a shotgun. 'And I know he came to see you at school. What did he say?'

'He just wanted to find out how you were. And then he asked about Hamish Willcock.'

'And what did you tell him?'

I have a feeling that any answer would be wrong. 'I told him you were fine and that Hamish was, you know … OK.'

'I thought I told you not to talk to him. What's the matter with you, Archie? Why are you trying to ruin my life?'

I know it's completely the wrong moment, but I have to say something. 'We need to talk about Dinger. He's not happy at Mrs Watt's house.'

Izzy's checking her phone again. 'Well, at least he's not getting cat hairs all over my clothes.'

'You don't understand, Wizz. He's really missing us.'

'No, he's not,' she says, scrolling angrily. 'So long as she's feeding him, he'll be fine. Cats don't care about anything but themselves.'

'What like you, you mean?'

Izzy shrugs. 'What are you going to do anyway, catnap him? You know we're not allowed pets.'

I've been thinking about that. 'There are some old garages around the back of Manton House. We could keep him there.'

'It's *not* going to happen,' says Izzy, stabbing the bus bell with her index finger. 'So stop going on about it. And stop trying to ruin my life.'

But things get even worse when we walk into Room 102. The curtains are drawn (well as far as they'd go) and it smells more terrible than ever.

Izzy clicks on the light. 'What are *you* doing here, Mum? Why aren't you at work?'

Mum is lying in bed. She hasn't even bothered to change out of her uniform. 'I was feeling a bit groggy so they sent me home.'

'And how are you now?' says Izzy.

'Not so great, to be honest. But all I need is a good night's sleep. There's a few bits and pieces in the fridge. You can get your own tea, can't you, love?'

'Yeah, course,' says Izzy.

'Hi Mum, how are you doing?' I say, trying to get a smile out of her. 'Do you want me to make you a cup of tea or something?'

She's definitely looking in my direction. But just for a second, I have this horrible feeling that she can't see me. That's not supposed to happen. According to Zofia, your family *never* loses sight of you.

'Mum, Mum, wake up. I need to tell you something about Dinger.'

She opens her eyes for a moment.

And then closes them again.

'Please Mum. I know you think all this is your fault. But it isn't, I promise.' Perhaps the tear that just splashed onto her face will keep her listening. 'We need you, Mum. We need you more than ever – not just Dinger, me and Izzy too. But I'm really scared that you've just given up.'

'Archie,' she whispers. 'Archie, is that you?'

A moment later, she's asleep.

'Mum, Mum, wake up. We have to do something about—'

'She doesn't want to hear about your stupid cat,' says Izzy. 'So stop bothering her. Or do you want to ruin Mum's life too?' She slams the fridge door in disgust. 'There's nothing in here anyway. I'm going for a bath.'

She's so keen to make a dramatic exit that she leaves her phone on top of the fridge. I can't believe how mean she was about Dinger. All she cares about are her stupid fake photos and trying to make me more miserable. And I'm so furious with her that a really horrible idea pops into my head. I mean, you could say it's her own fault. She should have been far more careful about hiding her password: cl1ntluvsizzy4eva.

OK, so it's kind of my fault too. But she's the one who showed me how to use it and she shouldn't have called the best cat in the world 'stupid' – especially on a day like today. That's why it seems like the perfect way of getting back at her.

So I grab her phone, race down three flights of stairs to the front door and get a nice photo of the sign outside. (MANTON HOUSE: Abandon hope all ye who enter here.) And then race back up again and take a few tasty shots of 'Izzy Ebbs' new home': the stains on the wall, 'our new kitchen' (aka the microwave) and 'me and Mum's bed that's so cool you can even watch TV from it'.

And by the time Izzy realises her phone is missing, I've Snapchatted them to everyone on her contacts list.

'Hi Izzy,' I say innocently, as she stands scowling in the doorway with a towel on her head. 'I think you might have forgotten this.'

# 17

I was quite pleased with myself to begin with. But lying in the dark while the people in the next room throw plates (or maybe frozen sausages?) at each other, I'm starting to realise that nothing has changed. Getting revenge on my sister won't help me escape from Manton House, make me visible again or get Dinger back. In fact, I already feel really bad about it. I know Izzy's only being nasty because she hates it here and she misses Clint. And she certainly doesn't deserve to have all her school friends laughing at her.

Maybe I could Snapchat all her contacts and tell them it was just a joke. Too late. There's no way I'll get hold of her phone again. She's so desperate for new messages that she's taken it to bed with her. I have *literally* no idea what to do. But I can't stay just lie here. Not with my sister's accusing snoring making me guiltier by the second. So at 12.27 by Mum's alarm clock, I throw off my summer duvet and hurry down to the basement.

‘I thought you said you’d be better off on your own, Archie.’

‘Well, maybe I was wrong.’

Zofia puts down her book. ‘What’s the matter, Archie? Are you OK?’

‘No, I’m not actually. I hate being invisible. I’ve just done something *completely* terrible to my sister and I’m really missing my cat.’

Zofia nods sympathetically. ‘Reksio had to stay in Poland. He’s such a cute dog, Archie. I cried for a week.’

‘We had to leave Dinger at our neighbour’s house,’ I say, knowing that if I start crying again I’ll never be able to stop. ‘But I went round to see him the other day, and he looks really thin, like he’s not eating properly. And I’m sure he’s scared of her horrible cats. So I’ve got this plan to get him back.’

‘Really?’

‘I haven’t *quite* worked out how to do it yet. I’m waiting for the right time.’

Zofia goes all quiet for a moment, wrinkling her forehead and biting on her bottom lip. And I’m pretty sure she’s going to say something sensible like, *your cat will be much better off with a responsible adult, so forget about it*, until her face bursts into an excited smile.

'That's a great idea, Archie. I could help you if you like.'

Zofia's pretty annoying. On the other hand, she's probably the one person in the world who understands what I'm going through right now. But why's she's being so nice to me?

'*Could* you?'

'Deffo,' says Zofia, practically breaking into a dance routine. 'And being invisible could actually be useful for a change.'

And just when things are starting to look more hopeful, a horrible thought pops into my head. 'But what if Dinger can't see me anymore?'

'Dinger's part of your family, of course he'll be able to see you,' says Zofia. 'So you'd better tell me about your plan, Archie. And then when the time comes, we'll be ready.'

'Do you know what, I think you're right, Zofia. You were right about something else too.'

'Yeah, probably,' she says with a 'modest' smile. 'What are you talking about, Archie?'

'We *have* got a lot in common, haven't we? We're both invisible, we both live at Manton

House and we're both animal lovers! And maybe you're right about sticking together at school. It couldn't be any worse than being invisible on my own!'

# 18

Izzy is in such a good mood this morning that we almost miss the bus.

'At last,' she says, scrolling through her phone at the speed of light. 'I knew it would work in the end.'

She's making me nervous. I haven't seen her this happy since the day of that famous school orchestra practice when she asked 'the hottest boy in the violin section' if he wanted to walk home with her ('plus maybe get some chips') *and he actually said yes!*

'What *are* you talking about, Izzy?'

'This is so great,' she says, smiling at the bus driver (which is weird in itself) and flashing her bus pass. 'Who's the loser now, eh, Courtney?'

And I have a really bad feeling as I sit down next to her. 'I don't know what you mean.'

'It started last night, Arch. And it's still happening this morning.'

'*What's* still happening?'

'Everyone's been Snapchatting me about the new house.'

It just slips out. 'I'm *really* sorry, Izzy.'

'What do you mean, sorry?' she says, laughing gleefully as another photo arrives. 'This is brilliant. Now everyone thinks we live in a big posh house, I won't have to worry anymore.'

'So you mean—'

'They loved the photos. I can't believe it took them so long.'

'Really?'

'That is so cute,' she says, handing me her phone. 'What do you think, Arch?'

A smiley girl in a red dress is standing in front of enormous fridge with a small dog under her arm. ('Nice gaff, babe. Lovin the new kitchen!!!)

A few seconds later, she disappears.

Sometimes I wish *I* could disappear in front of my sister. 'Yeah, nice. But don't say anything about it at school, Wizz. I mean … it's probably best if you … like … keep quiet and don't boast about it or anything.'

'Yeah, course' says Izzy, grabbing back her phone. 'No one likes a try hard.'

'Cool,' I say, glancing round at the back of the bus, so she won't notice how relieved I am.

'Hey, Archie,' says Zofia, who's sitting in the seat behind us with a wicked smile on her face. 'Does your sister like insects?'

'Shhhhh.'

'It's all right, she can't see me,' says Zofia, walking her fingers up the back of Izzy's neck. '*Incy wincy spider climbed up the water spout.*'

'Stop it,' I say, still feeling really guilty about the photos.

'Stop what?' says Izzy, brushing furiously the back of her neck.

'I mean the bus, Wizz. This is where I get off.'

'Push the bell yourself, you lazy toad,' says Izzy, already engrossed again in her phone. 'School's going to be well sick today. Just wait until I catch up with Courtney. By the time I've finished with her she'll be toast.'

Zofia is right behind her pulling a wide-mouthed frog face.

'Please don't do that,' I say.

'Why not?' says Izzy. 'It'll serve her right for all the times she's been horrible about me.'

'Come on,' says Zofia, pushing the bell. 'Are you ready for this, Archie?'

'Yeah, definitely.'

'Exactly,' says Izzy. 'I mean *she* started it when she said all those horrible things about Clinton's hair.'

'See you later,' I say, jumping up and following Zofia to the door.

'Bye, Archie,' calls Izzy, staring lovingly into her phone, like it's a magic mirror in a fairy tale. 'Have a great day now.'

After we've self-registered on the interactive white board, we both sit down at our normal tables. No one talks to us, of course. But it doesn't seem to matter so much anymore. I can turn round and chat with Zofia whenever I like. And I don't even get told off for it.

'So what are we waiting for?' I ask. 'When are we going to have some fun?'

'In a minute,' says Zofia. 'Mr Blott's going to take round his book-safe thingy. I just want to see how much money we've raised.'

I can't help laughing. 'Why would you want to do that? There's no point going to the party anyway. Two invisible kids on an inflatable assault course! Like you said, it's a health-and-safety nightmare.'

'Don't be such a snowflake,' says Zofia. 'Being invisible in a water fight would be awesome.'

'I thought you hated that sort of thing.'

'I said I hated PE, Archie. And that's because I never got picked for anything – even before I was invisible.'

A wave of sadness washes over me. 'I used to get picked for everything until we moved to Manton House.'

'OK, so who's got some lovely dosh for me?' says Mr Blott, brandishing his 'special version' of *Les Miserables*. 'Any more for any more?'

Chelsey waves a note with the queen's head on it. 'Me and my sister went without sweets for *three* days. We've raised twenty pounds.'

'We should have done a sponsored disappearance,' says Zofia. 'I bet no one thought of that.'

'Nice job, Chelsey,' says Mr Blott, giving *Les Miserables* a good shake. 'Well, that sounds pretty healthy, doesn't it, guys? I'd say that's mainly paper money, wouldn't you?'

'And we sold out of our slime in about half an hour,' says Caitlin. 'So then we had a penalty shootout in my back garden and Mum made everyone mocktails.'

'It was the best time ever,' says Josh. 'My dad's written you a cheque.'

'Excellent work, guys. You're well on the way to getting that inflatable obstacle course.'

'*And* the massive water fight,' shouts virtually everyone in the class including Zofia.

Mr Blott smiles. 'Yes, yes, and the water fight.'

'How much have we got?' says Amir.

Mr Blott returns *Les Miserables* to the pile of books on his desk and pretends to calculate the total by counting on his fingers. 'Well, after today's contributions, I'd say ... we only need to raise about ten more pounds.'

'Sweet,' says Callum Critchlow. 'That's nearly enough for a PS4.'

'Shut up, Callum,' says Caitlin, who's never liked him since he accidentally spilt paint on her in Year Four. 'No one wants to hear your stupid voice anyway.'

‘OK, guys, let’s settle down, shall we?’ says Mr Blott, as a row of maths problems appear on the whiteboard. ‘Now today, we’re going to be doing some work on probability.’

‘Hey Zofia,’ I say, already chuckling at the brilliant idea that’s just popped into my head. ‘Why don’t I grab Mr Blott’s book safe and make it fly around the classroom, like in a horror movie?’

Zofia rolls her eyes at me. ‘We don’t want to frighten people, Archie. We just want to have fun. If we start doing weird stuff like that they’ll probably shut the school down or something.’

‘So what *shall* we do?’

‘Whatever we like,’ says Zofia, slipping out of her seat. ‘The school is our oyster.’

And Caitlin is making a mean joke about the probability of Callum not ending up outside Mrs Goodall’s office before lunchtime (‘about a million to one’) as I follow Zofia to the door.

I’ve always wanted to see inside the staffroom. Unfortunately, it’s not quite as interesting as I thought it would be: just a few old chairs, some notices about health and safety and the arrangements for the Year Four trip to the mosque. But it *is* quite funny to find out some of the teachers' first names (*Benjamin* Blott, *Sharon* Goodall) and considering how much they go on about healthy eating, the contents of their packed lunches is quite interesting too!

But after we've put our feet up for a bit and microwaved a sachet of popcorn we run down the corridor to the headteacher's office. Sharon Goodall is on the phone to an angry parent, so Zofia stands behind her making little devil's horns with her fingers while I check out the photos on her desk.

'These must be her children,' I say, pointing at two smiling kids pushing a trolley through the wall on platform nine-and-three quarters. 'I thought she hated children.'

'Can you imagine it?' says Zofia, launching into a pretty good impression of our beloved headteacher. 'Don't run in the bathroom, Olivia. I'm not angry, Harry – just disappointed. All right, you two, that's a warning!'

The funny thing is when we stop to listen to the *real* Mrs Goodall, she actually sounds quite human.

'Yes, I know Callum's behaviour can be quite challenging at times ... and I'm sorry you feel that way. But I have a duty of care to *all* the children in my school. And permanent exclusion is only ever the very last resort.'

'Come on,' says Zofia. 'There's something I want to show you.'

Mr Messy the caretaker is cleaning the door handles in the corridor with his antibacterial spray.

'Oh dear, oh dear,' he mutters. 'Ten fifty-seven already and I still haven't dusted the photocopier.'

'Let's follow him,' says Zofia. 'There's something really funny I want you to see.'

I thought Mum was fussy – at least she used to be before we moved to Manton House – but Mr Messy makes her look like the untidiest person on the planet. On the front of his cleaning trolley are two plastic containers for collecting the recycling: green for waste paper and cardboard; yellow for plastics, wood, metal and glass. So, after he's dusted the photocopier, unblocked the boys' toilets, checked the school field for dog poo and carried Mrs Goodall's life-sized model of the queen to the hall ('for my assembly about always doing your best'), we trail him around the school in search of single-use plastics, milk cartons, scrap paper, jam jars, yoghurt cartons, old highlighter pens and a load of scrunched-up diet coke cans from the staffroom.

But he looks kind of guilty when he gets to the library and, taking some books from the bottom of his cleaning trolley, slips quietly inside.

'Wait until you see *this*,' says Zofia.

'What's he up to anyway?'

'Everything in its proper place, Lionel,' he whispers to himself, as he takes out *Charlie and the Chocolate Factory* and puts it back on the shelf next to *The Cat in the Hat*.

And I suddenly realise what he's doing. 'Oh, I get it. He's putting them all back in alphabetical order.'

Zofia nods. 'Are you thinking what I'm thinking?'

I know it's a bit mean, but I have to admit, it is pretty funny too. Every time he goes to collect some more books we run round changing their places on the shelves. Mr Messy looks extremely confused. But he keeps trying to restore order until we start putting non-fiction books in the fiction section and it all gets too much for him.

'*Stig of the Dump* next to *My First Encyclopaedia*?' he says, fanning his glowing cheeks with *The Boy in the Dress*. 'You've *definitely* been working too hard, Lionel. Time for a nice cup of tea.'

# 19

Caitlin obviously got the odds about right. Seven minutes before lunchtime, Callum Critchlow is already sitting outside Mrs Goodall's office.

'Well, that's a bit sad,' says Zofia. 'Why's everyone mean so about him?'

'You are joking, aren't you?'

I always try to keep at least an arm's length away from Callum. You never know what he might have up his sleeve. (Tomato sauce sachets? Water bombs?) But Zofia sits down in the empty chair next to him.

'Ughh, look at that. He's got yoghurt stains all over his sweatshirt.'

'Yes,' I say, still keeping my distance. 'Probably because he's been throwing it at people.'

'Well, *I* like him' says Zofia, softly dabbing at Callum's yoghurt stains with a scrunched-up tissue. 'He's about the only person who was nice to me when I first arrived.'

'If you say so, Zofia. But can we get some food now? I'm starving.'

The good thing about being invisible is that you never have to queue for anything. No one sees us walk into the hall five minutes early, serve ourselves double portions of ham pizza, herby, diced potatoes, chocolate sponge and custard and wolf them down in world-record time.

'Do you think they'll ever see me again?' I say, the knot in my stomach tightening as Caitlin, Josh and Amir sit down at our favourite table by the window.

'I don't know. Maybe,' says Zofia. 'Let's go over and join them, shall we?'

'Do we have to?'

'It might be a laugh,' says Zofia. 'Oh, come on. I've never seen them close up before.'

It's small consolation, but at least they haven't replaced me with Archie 2.0 yet. There's still an empty place on the end that's just about big enough for me and Zofia.

You'd think that hanging out with your old friends would be good fun. But it's not actually that great when none of them can see you. At least they've started rebuilding Awesomeopolis. The trouble is no one remembers who designed the 24-hour Candy Floss and Pizza Bar and it's so frustrating that I can't remind them it was me.

And Amir won't stop talking about his new movie script. '*The Cabbage Strikes Back* is the best thing I've ever written. And Boris Broccoli is, like, the greatest villain ever.'

Caitlin is still having a go at Callum Critchlow. 'What a loser, eh? Did you see what he did with that yoghurt? He shouldn't be at this school anyway. Old Goodall should have permanently excluded him ages ago.'

'That's not very nice,' says Zofia. 'I don't think much of your friend, Archie.'

'Caitlin's OK sometimes,' I say, not quite sure why I'm sticking up for her. 'She was pretty kind to me when I broke my arm. She gave me the login for her dad's Netflix.'

I can just about cope with Caitlin being mean and Amir the film critic, but when Josh stops guzzling chocolate pudding for a moment and announces, 'Hey guys, want to hear my new joke?' I don't think I can take it anymore.

'What's the matter, Archie?' says Zofia. 'You've

gone all red in the face. I thought you liked jokes.'

'Go on, Joshy,' says Caitlin. 'Let's hear it then.'

'Doctor, doctor,' says Josh. 'There's a man in the waiting room who says he can make himself invisible.'

And my heart sinks to the bottom of the deepest ocean.

Josh is already howling with laughter. 'And the doctor says … ha, ha, ha, ha … the doctor says, "Tell him I can't see him right now!"'

It's a pretty offensive joke if you happen to be invisible. Even so, that's the least of my worries. I mean it's bad enough that Caitlin and Amir obviously think it's the funniest thing since 'thingy'-shaped vegetables. But I'll tell you what I'm really angry about. It's not Josh's joke in the first place.

IT'S ONE OF MINE.

Maybe this is how Callum Critchlow feels. I'm so furious that I just can't control myself. Because the next thing I know I've pushed half a bowl of chocolate pudding and cold custard straight into Josh's lap.

'Urghhhhhhhh,' says Josh. But at least he isn't laughing anymore.

'Looks like you've wet yourself,' says Caitlin,

who *is* still laughing.

'Or worse,' adds Amir.

'Archie, wait,' calls Zofia, as I jump up from my seat and start running. 'Slow down. I can't keep up with you.'

But I don't stop.

'What's up? I thought we were having fun.'

'We were,' I say, speeding past the KS1 nurture area. 'But I hate it that they can't see me – not even online! My whole life's a complete mess.'

Zofia grabs my arm and manages to slow me to a halt. 'Calm down, Archie. It can't be that bad.'

'Oh yes, it is. Mum hardly talks to me anymore and I'm really missing Clint.'

'Who's Clint?'

'My sister's boyfriend. You'd like him. He's great.'

Zofia smiles and puts her hand on my shoulder. 'Cheer up, Archie. You'll feel much better when we get Dinger back. Have you got everything?'

'Yes. I found some cat treats in my old football shorts.'

Zofia wrinkles her nose in disgust. 'Looks like we're good to go. Like you said, all we've got to do now is wait for the right moment.'

'Yeah … 'spose so,' I shrug. 'But I think I need to be on my own for a bit. Maybe I'll pop outside for ten minutes. Catch you later, Zofia.'

Until now I thought that things couldn't possibly get any worse, but then I walk out of Main Reception and see a familiar figure prowling around the playground like a bloodthirsty lion.

'What are *you* doing here?' I ask. 'You do know it's only lunchtime?'

Izzy doesn't answer. She just stares at me, her puffy red eyes brimming with hatred.

'It was you, wasn't it, Archie? How could you *do* that to me?'

# 20

'I have no idea what you're talking about, Wizz.'

'You're the only one who knew about it,' she says, jabbing me in the chest with her shiny red fingernail. 'And you're the only one who knows my password.'

'So what?

'Don't try and act all innocent. I know what you did, Archie. And I'll never forgive you.'

'But I—'

'All you had to do was keep your mouth shut. You know how much I hate that place. So why did you have to send photos of it to all my friends?'

'Because you were mean about Dinger,' I mumble. 'And you won't help me to get him back.'

She stares down at the hopscotch court. She can't even look at me. 'Just listen to yourself, Archie. We're living in a hostel for homeless people. And now my whole school knows about it. But all you care about is your stupid cat.'

‘He’s really unhappy, Izzy. I’m not even allowed to see him anymore.’

‘I heard them talking about it in Citizenship – Izzy Ebbs and her “posh” new house. They thought it was *so* funny.’

‘I bet they didn’t.’

‘I don’t care about that lot anyway,’ said Izzy, who obviously does. ‘But when Clint finds out – that’s if he doesn’t know already – he’ll never want to see me again.’

‘I’m really sorry, Izzy. I didn’t mean to—’

‘Just leave me alone, OK.’ She spins round and heads for the bus stop.

I can barely keep up with her. ‘Please. I know it was stupid but—’

‘I don’t want to talk to you. I don’t want to see you. I don’t want to have *anything* to do with you. As far as I’m concerned, Archie, you don’t even exist.’

# 21

The next morning, Izzy still won't talk to me. So when I get to school, I spend the first few lessons snoozing in the library with Zofia. Having fun is the last thing on my mind. Not now that one of the few people in the world who can actually see me is acting like I'm not even there.

In fact, I'm so fed up that when Mr Messy pops in at first break with a few books, I can't even be bothered to mess about with the order.

'Come on, Archie,' says Zofia. 'She's your sister. She can't stay mad at you for long.'

'You don't know Izzy. That time I thought her stupid face cream was squeezy cheese, she wouldn't talk to me for a week.'

Zofia yawns. 'Let's go down to the classroom for a bit. I'm getting bored.'

The first thing that hits me is the silence. Mr Blott's lessons never get out of hand, but there's nearly always someone laughing. So we stand at the back, trying to figure it out.

'I don't get it,' says Zofia. 'Do you think it's one of Mr Blott's games?'

'I don't think so, Zofia. Look at his face.'

I've never seen him like this before. Mr Blott looks furious. His eyes are blazing and his voice as cold as ice. 'I want you all to listen very carefully, 6B. Something extremely serious has happened.'

'Has Callum been buying yoghurt again?' says Josh, proving once and for all that he definitely shouldn't try to be funny.

'Be quiet, Joshua,' says Mr Blott. 'I'm in no mood for your feeble jokes.'

Zofia doesn't need to whisper, but I suppose it just feels right.

'I don't like the sound of this, Archie. What's going on?'

'I have no idea.'

'It's disappeared,' says Mr Blott. 'The money you raised for the Leavers' Party. It's … gone.'

The whole class holds its breath.

'It was here first thing this morning because I

counted it. But I've looked everywhere, and the book safe with money in it has … disappeared.'

'So what's happened to it then?' says Chelsey.

'You probably put it down somewhere,' says Amir.

Mr Blott shakes his head and stands staring into mid-air until the words finally leak out. 'I'm afraid to say there's only one possible explanation. Someone must have taken it.'

'Yeah, the honey monster,' says Callum.

Mr Blott is so angry he's beyond shouting. 'It's not funny, Callum. You'd all raised a lot of money.'

Most of the class is really angry too.

'I sold thirty-two friendship bracelets.'

'My mum says the whole house stinks of slime.'

'And I went without chocolate for *three whole days*!'

'All right, all right, that's enough,' says Mr Blott. 'Now I don't want to jump to any conclusions. But there's something else.'

Everyone goes quiet again – apart from Callum.

'You've won the lottery and you're taking us all to Alton Towers.'

Mr Blott hesitates. It's almost like he doesn't want to say it.

'You guys were the only ones who knew about the money. So ... it looks like the person who took the money must have been someone in 6B.'

Caitlin has her hand up.

'Yes, Caitlin. What is it?' says Mr Blott.

'There's no point wasting time looking for it,' she says. 'We all know what must have happened.'

Mr Blott runs his hand through his cool spiky hair. 'Look, if you know something about this, Caitlin. I think you'd better speak up now.'

'Well, it's obvious, isn't it?' she says, pointing at the boy with the yoghurt-stained sweatshirt. 'Callum took it. It's most probably under his bed! That's if he hasn't spent it already.'

'No, I never,' says Callum. 'What's she saying *that* for?'

Zofia is the first to jump to his defence. 'I bet he didn't do it, Archie. Callum's not like that.'

But a murmur of agreement is already running around the classroom.

Luckily for Callum, Mr Blott obviously agrees with Zofia. 'Calm down, Callum. No one is accusing you of anything.'

'Yes, we are,' says a voice from the back.

'Well, I'm not,' says Mr Blott. 'If Callum says he knows nothing about it, I believe him.'

But by the time we follow Mr Blott to Mrs Goodall's office at lunchtime, he doesn't sound quite so certain.

'Well, it's *possible*, I suppose. But I really don't think it's Callum's style. I know he can be … challenging sometimes. But underneath he's got a heart of gold.'

Mrs Goodall takes a bite of her reduced-calorie tuna and sweetcorn sandwich. 'And you've definitely looked everywhere?'

'Yes, of course.'

'Look, I know you always like to see the best in people, Ben. But if all roads lead to Callum Critchlow, you'll have to ask him about it, I'm afraid.'

Mr Blott sighs. 'You know what a hard time he's having at the moment. This could put him back months.'

'Well yes,' says Mrs Goodall, reaching for her

diet coke. 'But I've had more complaints about Callum Critchlow than any other child in the school. Some of the parents are just itching for me to exclude him. If we don't investigate this properly, it'll be all over Facebook.'

'That is so unfair,' says Zofia. 'Callum always gets the blame for everything.'

'Well, who *did* take it then?' I say, wondering if I can sneak a sip of her coke while Mrs Goodall isn't looking.

'Just leave it with me for a bit,' says Mr Blott. 'I'm sure I can get to the bottom of this.'

At the end of the afternoon, we slip into the back of the classroom for Mr Blott's important announcement.

'Do you think he's found it, Archie?' says Zofia.

'From the look on his face, I'd say *definitely* not.'

Mr Blott waits for complete silence. It doesn't take long. 'OK, guys, listen up. As things stand, it looks like you're not going to get your inflatable obstacle course.'

'Oh well,' says Callum cheerfully. 'At least we can still have the massive water fight.'

Mr Blott shakes his head. 'I'm afraid not.'

'You're joking,' says Zofia. 'I was looking forward to that.'

'In fact,' says Mr Blott. 'It looks like there's not going to be a party at all.'

Caitlin has her hand up, but she doesn't wait to be asked to speak. 'That's *so* not fair. We've worked really hard for it. It's not our fault "someone's" stolen the money.'

'Quiet, Caitlin. I haven't finished yet.' Mr Blott starts pacing the classroom. 'I've had a long think about it, and there *might* be a way you could still have your party.'

Practically everyone in the class has their hand in the air.

'You see, someone here knows what happened to that money. I'm not asking you to say anything now – you can come and find me in the staffroom or speak to Mrs Goodall if you like. But if that person – or *persons*,' he adds quickly, 'comes forward by the end of school tomorrow, we've decided that the party can still go ahead.'

'And what if no one *does*?' says Amir.

Mr Blott stops pacing. 'Well, if we don't hear anything, the party will be cancelled. And Mrs Goodall will probably have to contact the police.'

Caitlin is the first person to break the stunned silence. 'Well. go on, Callum. Do the right thing for once. Tell Mr Blott what you did with that money.'

'Shut up, shut up, shut up,' says Callum, his hands clasped tightly over his ears. 'I never took it, OK?'

'Stop ruining it for everyone else,' says Caitlin. 'Tell Mr Blott where you've hidden that money.'

'Look, I didn't do it,' says Callum, sweeping pencil pots from the table and stumbling to the door. 'I swear on my dad's life.'

But I can't help thinking that running off like that is a pretty good clue that he *did*. 'So what do you reckon, Zofia? Still think Callum's innocent?'

'Yes, probably,' she says, taking my hand and dragging me to the door. 'But there's only one way to find out.'

# 22

'I've never been in one of these things before,' says Zofia. 'The fold-down seats are so cool.'

Callum hasn't said a word since we followed him across the playground and jumped into the back of his taxi.

'Bit quiet today, aren't we?' says the taxi driver. 'What's the matter, bad day at the office?'

'Yeah,' whispers Callum.

'That's not like you, matey,' says the taxi driver. 'I thought you loved a good yoghurt fight!'

'Yeah, I do.' whispers Callum.

'Why are we doing this anyway?' I say, half wishing I'd caught the bus. 'We're both invisible. What's it got to do with us?'

'It's not fair that Callum gets blamed for everything,' says Zofia. 'I just want to prove to you that he didn't take that money.'

'And then what?' I say, glancing out the window at the skateboard park where Top Table Productions filmed the exploding strawberry sequence. 'Even if he didn't take it, it's not like we can tell anyone.'

Zofia shrugs. 'I don't know yet. What's the matter with you anyway? You look like you're going to puke.'

She's right. A sickly mixture of herby dried potatoes and custard is bubbling away nastily in my stomach.

'I didn't know Callum lived round here. I wish I'd never come.'

'Why not?'

'Nearly home, matey,' says the taxi driver. 'What are you doing tonight?'

'The usual,' says Callum.

I'm not sure if I can bear to look. But in the end I just can't help myself.

'Because this is where we used to live,' I say, pointing at the For Sale sign. 'And that's our old house.'

A couple of minutes later, the taxi pulls up beside a blue gate and Callum jumps out.

'See you tomorrow, matey,' calls the taxi driver. 'And cheer up. It may never happen!'

The house looks exactly the same as 22 Station Road, apart from the handrail and concrete ramp leading up to the front door. Callum takes a key from his pocket and turns it in the lock.

'Hello, Dad,' he calls. 'I'm home.'

We follow him past the wheelchair in the hallway and a photo of a frowning Callum dressed up as the Cat in the Hat, into the lounge.

'All right, Cal?' says the man on the sofa. 'How was school?'

'I don't want to talk about it,' says Callum, throwing his rucksack on the floor.

'*That's* who it is!' I say, pointing at the man on the sofa. 'I wondered who he was.'

'What are you talking about, Archie?' says Zofia.

'I saw Callum down at the council offices. He was pushing a man in a wheelchair. It must have been his dad.'

Zofia nods. 'I think he has to look after him sometimes.'

'Calm down, Cal,' says his dad. 'So what have you been up to this time?'

'Nothing, that's the whole point,' says Callum. 'Look, I'll tell you later, Dad. I need to tidy up a bit and do the hoovering.'

I check the front window for the alien spaceship that's abducted the old Callum and replaced him with this weird hoovering version. 'So what are we going to do now, Zofia?'

'Search the house for *Les Miserables*, of course. If Callum took Mr Blott's book safe, it shouldn't be that difficult to find. You do upstairs, and I'll check down here.'

I don't like snooping through other people's stuff, especially when someone's following me round with an antibacterial spray and a vacuum cleaner. But it's all in a good cause, I suppose. So I check inside the back of the toilet (like I've seen on TV cop shows) and go through the pile of books by the side of Callum's dad's bed. Most of them are detective stories, plus *The Multiple Sclerosis Cookbook* and *Mindfulness for Beginners*. But there's definitely no sign of *Les Miserables*.

'Have you found anything?' shouts Zofia.

'No nothing. What about you?'

'Course not,' calls Zofia. 'So I'm going to clean up the kitchen for a bit.'

Callum starts work on the bath and I slip into his bedroom. It's a bit like *my* old room, but not so tidy. A superhero on the wall, a photo of Callum and his dad at Alton Towers, Lego all over the floor, and, oh look, we've even read some of the same books. But still no sign of *Les Mis*.

And I've pretty much decided that Zofia must be right when I remember what Caitlin said. *He's most probably hiding it under the bed*. So I kneel down and have a look.

'Oh no, I don't believe it.'

I suppose I shouldn't be surprised. I shouldn't really be upset either. But unlike me, Callum Critchlow has managed to keep Stretch Armstrong in one piece. And for some reason, this really hurts.

'So now do you believe me?' says Zofia, who's sitting next to Callum's dad on the sofa watching *Escape to the Country*.

'I suppose so,' I say. 'But he could have left it anywhere, couldn't he? I mean he could have dumped it in the sea for all we know.'

'He didn't take that money, Archie. You know he didn't.'

Callum looks much happier when he arrives

from the kitchen with a mug of tea and a plate of chocolate fingers. 'Thanks for doing the washing up, Dad. You *must* be feeling better.'

'Don't know what you're talking about, son. I've been sat in front of the gogglebox all day.'

But Callum's still smiling. 'Yeah, course you have, Dad.'

'So come on, Cal,' says Mr Critchlow, reaching for a chocolate finger. 'What happened at school today?'

'Not now, Dad. I need to get started on our tea.'

It's *The Chase* in a minute,' says Mr Critchlow. 'I've been on my own all day, Callum. You are going to watch it with me, aren't you?'

'Yeah … course.'

'Good. So, sit down, son, and tell me what you're so upset about.'

Zofia jumps up from the sofa as Callum takes her place.

'It's nothing, Dad. Don't worry about it.'

'But I do worry,' says Mr Critchlow, sucking the chocolate off his biscuit first, just like I do. 'Come on, spit it out, Cal. You'll feel better once you've told me.'

Callum doesn't look nearly so frightening at

home. And I don't think I've ever seen him cry before.

'You remember that money we were raising for the Leavers' Party?'

'How could I forget?' says his dad with a knowing smile. 'We made twenty jars of marmalade. How many did you manage to sell in the end?'

'Nine,' says Callum. 'The rest are in the cupboard, Dad.'

'Well, that's not bad, Cal. I shouldn't worry about it.'

'Sounds pretty good to me,' says Zofia, who's lying on the carpet doing weird yoga exercises. 'Do *you* know how to make marmalade, Archie?'

'Well, I—'

'No, Dad, it's not that,' says Callum, wiping his nose on his school sweatshirt. 'Mr Blott keeps all the money in this secret book-safe thing.'

'Sounds cool,' says Mr Critchlow. 'Like James Bond, eh?'

Callum nods. 'Yeah, but it's disappeared, Dad. So now we can't have the party.'

'That's a shame. You were looking forward to that inflatable assault course, weren't you, Cal?'

But Callum can't speak anymore. His

shoulders are shaking and all he can manage is a strange sobbing sound.

'Don't worry, mate,' says his dad. 'It'll probably turn up in the end. And even if it doesn't, there are plenty of other ways to have fun. You should know that!'

'You … don't … understand,' sobs Callum. 'Everyone thinks that I stole it – even Mr Blott. But I … I didn't, I swear. You believe me, don't you, Dad?'

Mr Critchlow doesn't even hesitate. 'Course I do, Cal,' he says, wrapping his around him and pulling him close. 'You might get a bit overexcited sometimes, but I know you'd never do something like that.'

'What about you, Archie,' says Zofia. 'Do you believe him?'

And I've never been more sure of anything in my life.

'Yes.'

'Good,' says Zofia, jumping up from the carpet. 'Then my work here is done. Come on, Archie, let's leave them to it.'

And the theme tune of *The Chase* is just starting as we slip quietly out of the front door.

'Hurry up, Archie. If we get move on, we might catch the next bus.'

But I've just had a *much* better idea. 'You are joking, aren't you, Zofia?'

'I didn't think I was, Archie. So why are you smiling like that?'

'Because it's the moment we've been waiting for,' I say, checking the front pocket of my rucksack to make sure I haven't forgotten anything. 'We're ten minutes' walk from my old house and *The Chase* is on. It's the perfect time to rescue Dinger.'

# 23

'Follow me,' I say, sick with excitement as we race down the passage at the side of Mrs Watts' house.

'Wait up,' says Zofia. 'No one can see us remember. We can take our time.'

'I'm going to get my cat back, Zofia. I don't *want* to take my time!'

An army of gnomes stand guard over Mrs Watt's garden. But not even fifty little men with white beards and fishing rods can stop me now. So I push open the back door and we step into the kitchen.

'I can't believe she leaves it unlocked,' says Zofia, stepping over three half-eaten bowls of cat food. 'Someone should warn her about that.'

'We've only got about five minutes,' I say. 'As soon as *The Chase* is over, she'll want another cup of tea. Let's find Dinger and get him out of here.'

Zofia is checking out the photos of Mrs Watts' grandchildren on the fridge. 'Look at them, Archie. Don't they look cute?'

'Never mind that. Do you remember the plan?'

'It's not exactly rocket science,' says Zofia, who's spelled out 'GIRL POWER' with the little magnetic letters on the fridge door. 'You hide Dinger under your sweatshirt, I open the front door and we leg it back to the bus stop.'

'But we've got to find him first,' I say, reaching into my pocket for the packet of cat treats. 'These are perfect. Dinger absolutely loves them.'

'I can't wait to meet him,' says Zofia, following me out to the gloomy hallway. 'This is so awesome, Archie. We're going to rescue Dinger!'

I get down on my hands and knees and crawl towards the sound of the television. Every few centimetres I place a disgusting-looking cat treat on the fading brown carpet. 'Dinger? Diiiiinger? Where are you, boy? It's me, Archie.'

'Dingy, Dingy, Dingy, Diiiiinger,' calls Zofia. 'Come out, come out, wherever you are.'

'Don't talk to him like that,' I say, crawling past the table with the old-fashioned telephone on it. 'You'll only confuse him.'

'He can't hear me anyway,' says Zofia. 'He's your cat, don't forget.'

There's one thing I'm still terrified about: what if I'm invisible to Dinger too? I know he's part of my family, but it's not like we're related by birth, is it? And there's no point taking him back to Manton House if he doesn't even know I'm there.

'Why have you stopped?' says Zofia. 'I thought you said we only had five minutes.'

'We have,' I say, staring in horror at what I've just seen sitting on the sofa. 'So what are we going to do now?'

'OMG,' whispers Zofia. 'I see what you mean.'

Bimbo and Mrs Thatcher are watching the dog next door from the windowsill and Mrs Watts looks totally gripped by her favourite programme. But that's not the problem. The problem is the ginger cat who's fast asleep on her lap.

'Dinger *must* be confused,' I say, tiptoeing towards him with my arms outstretched. 'He never falls asleep on anyone's lap.'

Zofia grabs my hand. 'You can't just pick him up, Archie. He'll look like he's flying!'

'OK, so what do we do then?'

'That one's easy,' says Zofia, pointing at the television. 'The answer's B: Albert Einstein.'

'I *said*, what do we do?'

'We'll have to wake Dinger,' says Zofia. 'You put down some more cat treats and I'll knock something over in the hall.'

Dinger can sleep through thunderstorms. I try getting closer and calling in his ear, but he doesn't even move. So I put a cat treat on edge of the sofa and start laying out a trail to the hall.

Zofia knocks a chair over.

'Louder,' I call. 'He's still fast asleep.'

'What about this?' says Zofia, opening and slamming the front door.

The television is turned up so loud that Mrs Watts doesn't look away for a second. But Dinger yawns, stretches and opens one eye. 'Better,' I shout. 'Try something else.'

Zofia tips over the umbrella stand; Dinger starts licking himself.

'Come on, boy,' I say, pushing a cat treat closer to his mouth. 'Let's get you out of here.'

Mrs Watts mumbles, 'I thought Kardashian was a place in Somerset,' but her eyes never leave the screen.

Dinger wolfs down his first cat treat and starts working his way to the hall.

I race out in front of him, so happy I could

almost cry. 'He's coming, Zofia. He's coming. Look.'

Dinger turns the corner and walks towards me.

'You see that, Zoff. He knows who I am!

But as soon as he gets to his final cat treat, he stops dead and refuses to come any closer. 'Come on, Dinger. You can see me, can't you, boy?'

Zofia is standing by the open door. 'Just pick him up, Archie. *The Chase* will be over in a sec.'

'Hang on a minute,' I say, making mewing sounds and rubbing my fingers and thumbs together. 'I just need to make sure he recognises me.'

'Come on, Archie. We haven't got time.'

The next five seconds are complete agony. I keep calling. But Dinger doesn't move.

'Hurry up,' says Zofia. 'That's the theme tune.'

But what happens next is the sweetest moment of all; the moment when Dinger looks up at me through his emerald-green eyes, meows 'hello' and starts rubbing himself against my legs. 'Told you so, didn't I, Zofia? He knows who I am, don't you, boy?'

Zofia's reply is not all what I'm expecting. It's a

strange kind of snarling sound. Less like a human and more like a … cat.

More like *two* cats.

Bimbo and Margaret Thatcher have polished off the rest of the cat treats and are standing side by side, barring the way to the front door.

'Just grab him, Archie,' calls Zofia. 'Come on.'

But it's too late. Mrs Thatcher growls and Bimbo bares his fangs.

Poor Dinger turns and runs. STRAIGHT INTO THE ARMS OF MRS WATTS.

'You naughty boy,' she says, smothering Dinger in kisses. 'Look what you've done to my umbrellas.' She smiles and holds him even tighter. 'I can see I'm going to have to keep a very close on eye you. But don't worry, Schrödinger. From now on, I'm never going to let you out of my sight.'

'Say something, Archie,' says Zofia, as the empty bus chugs slowly up the hill. 'You haven't said a word the whole way.'

'It's all my fault, isn't it? Now I'm never going to get Dinger back.'

'Of course you are,' says Zofia. 'You'll just have to wait a bit longer. We can work something out at school.'

'No, we can't.'

'Why not?'

Somewhere between the seafront and the top of the cliffs, I'd decided it was for the best. 'Because I'm not coming to school anymore.'

'Why not?' says Zofia.

'Because there's no point. I'm fed up with being invisible. And I hate it that all my friends have forgotten me.'

I'm expecting her to be a bit more sympathetic. But she just sounds angry.

'Don't be so selfish, Archie. Of course you're coming to school.'

'No. Why should I?'

'It's obvious, isn't it?' says Zofia. 'I need your help tomorrow.'

'Help with what?'

Zofia rolls her eyes at me. 'The only way of proving that Callum didn't take that money is to find out who did. We've got one more day or the Leavers' Party will be cancelled. Come on, Archie. I can't do it without you.'

I always thought she was a bit weird. Now I know for sure. 'Practically everyone in the school has got a grudge against him. Why are you so keen to help Callum?'

'Because he can't help himself,' says Zofia. 'Think about it, Archie. We know he's innocent. But whatever he says, no one's going to listen to him. In fact, he might as well be … *invisible*.' Zofia fixes me with her big brown eyes. 'And we both know what that feels like, don't we?'

I stare out the window, thinking of Dinger and his super-soft fur.

'Well, come on, Archie. Are you going to help me or not?'

I reach into my rucksack and pull out my homework diary. 'We should probably start by drawing up a list of suspects.'

# 24

Lunch break is nearly over. We've been trailing our 'prime suspects' around the school since assembly. And we're still getting absolutely nowhere.

Even Zofia sounds like she's starting to give up. 'I thought it would be so easy. If there's one job in the world where invisibility ought to be an advantage, it's being a detective.'

It hasn't helped us much so far. Zofia thinks that someone's trying to frame Callum and get him excluded. But we've listened to at least twenty private conversations – we've even followed Mason (Callum's latest wedgie victim) around the adventure trail – and we haven't got the slightest clue.

'I suppose we could try that girl in Year Five,' I say. 'You know, the one he pushed in the swimming pool.'

'What's the point?' says Zofia, casting her eyes along the line of dancers practising their new routine. 'Everyone thinks he took that money. No wonder Callum looks so fed up.'

It's true. Callum hasn't even got the energy for a yoghurt fight. He's sitting alone at a picnic bench, munching miserably on a raw carrot.

And believe it or not, I actually feel quite sorry for him. 'I've got an idea, Zofia. Why don't we send an anonymous letter to Mr Blott, saying we know that Callum's innocent?'

Zofia shakes her head, 'Because no one will believe us. We *have* to find out who took that money – it's the only way.'

And then I see something slightly suspicious. I mean, it's probably nothing. But, like I told you, we're getting desperate here. 'Well, that's strange.'

'What is it, Archie?'

I point across at the huge orange recycling bin. 'Over there, look.'

'What am I supposed to be looking at?'

If I didn't know Caitlin better, I wouldn't think anything of it. But ever since the beginning of Year One she's spent every minute of every break and lunchtime playing football. So why has she sneaked off behind the recycling bin with Amir?

'Those two, what do you think they're whispering about?'

'Probably some stupid film or that Boresomeopolis place.'

Zofia makes me laugh sometimes. 'Yeah, probably. But let's go and listen anyway.'

'I *had* to,' whispers Caitlin. 'Mum thinks he's getting really out of hand.'

'Are you sure it's a good idea, though?' says Amir. 'Isn't it a bit cruel?'

'I don't know, maybe,' says Caitlin. 'But Mum says it not fair on the rest of us. And if *I* don't do something about it, she will.'

Amir checks to see that no one's listening. 'So where have you hidden it?'

Caitlin is staring right into my eyes. 'Down in Mrs Goodall's conservation area – just until I can find a better place. But you mustn't tell anyone, not even Josh. We need to make sure that no one knows who—'

But before Caitlin can spill the beans, the bell goes and the whole school starts trooping back towards main reception.

'Are you thinking what I'm thinking?' says Zofia.

Caitlin's my friend. Well, she certainly used to be. So it's hard to believe she could do something so mean. But I've got to admit, she does look pretty guilty. 'Yes … yes, I think I might be.'

It looks like the only possible explanation, doesn't it?' says Zofia. 'Caitlin took the party money to get back at Callum. And now she's hidden it in the conservation area. We need to get down there straight away.'

But we're only halfway across the netball court when a curly-haired giant runs into the playground and starts shouting my name.

'Archie, Archie Ebbs, Archie, where are you?'

'Who's that?' says Zofia.

'It's my sister's boyfriend – *ex* boyfriend – Clint. You know the one I was telling you about.'

I start walking towards him, but Zofia pulls me back. 'We haven't got time, Archie. He won't be able to see you anyway.'

But she's wrong, he already has. 'Thank goodness I've found you, Arch. I *really* need your help.'

'Wait a minute,' I say, bumping the fist that he offers me. 'You can see me, can't you?'

Clint looks confused. 'Is this one of your jokes, Arch?'

'No, no it's just that—' I turn to Zofia. 'Why do you think he can see me?'

Zofia shrugs. 'You did say Clint was like family, didn't you?'

Clint looks even more confused. 'Who are you talking to, Arch?'

'No one, just...'

'Ask him what's the matter,' says Zofia. 'He looks really upset.'

Clint smiles at Zofia. (So I guess that means she's *kind of* family too.) 'Sorry, didn't see you there. You must be a friend of Archie's. And any friend of Archie's is a friend of mine.'

'Hi Clint. I'm Zofia.'

'And you're dead right, Zofia, I am upset,' says Clint, offering her his fist to bump. 'Something really terrible has happened.'

'What is it?' I say, hoping he's not going to ask me about Hamish Willcock again.

'It's Izzy,' says Clint. 'She's disappeared.'

My heart nearly stops beating and my hands turn to ice. 'So Wizz has turned invisible too. Is she with you now, Clint? Or is she still at school?'

It's the first time I've ever seen him look angry. 'It's not funny, Arch. You didn't see how upset she looked.'

'Why, what happened?' says Zofia.

'It was in computer science,' says Clint. 'Courtney Foden put some photos of that Manton House place on the whiteboard. Poor Izzer. If she didn't want anyone to know about it, I can't see why she sent them to everyone in the first place.'

'She didn't,' I say, feeling so guilty I almost wish I could really disappear. 'It was me.'

Clint looks confused again. 'But why did you–?'

'Never mind that,' says Zofia. 'Where is she now?'

'That's just it, Zofia. I have no idea. She told Courtney *exactly* what she thought of her and then ran off in floods of tears.' Clint looks like he's about to do the same thing. 'I'm so worried about her, Archie. We need to find her before she does something silly.'

'But how?' I say. 'I thought you had no idea where she was.'

Clint takes out his mobile. 'She sent me a text about half an hour ago. I thought you might know what it meant, Arch.'

*Need to chill for a bit. And you'll never find me. So don't even try. Goodbye Clinton. Izz xx*

'Let's go,' I say, already setting off towards the bus stop. 'I think I know where she is.'

Clint sets off after me. 'That's bangin', Arch. But don't you think you should tell a teacher where you're going?'

'It's OK,' I say. 'They won't miss me anyway.'

Zofia is running alongside me. 'I'm coming with you, Archie. We'll have more chance of finding her with the three of us.'

'What about the party money?'

'The money can wait,' says Zofia. 'We need to find your sister first.'

# 25

Between the library and the seafront it starts raining. Not pouring, but the kind of spittery-spattery stuff that Mum calls 'typical British holiday weather'.

'I wish you'd told me about it, Arch,' says Clint, glancing gloomily at the choppy sea. 'It must have been horrible.'

'Izzy wouldn't let me. She thought if you found out where we lived, you wouldn't want to go out with her anymore.'

'But I'm not like that, Archie. You know I'm not.'

'Of course I do.'

'She was probably all mixed up,' says Zofia. 'It's like that when you first move into Manton House.'

The bus crawls, coughing and spitting to the top of the hill. We pass the posh houses where Izzy took all the photos and I jump up and push the bell.

'OK, guys, we're here.'

'You sure about this?' says Clint following me and Zofia to the door. 'Izzer hates getting her hair wet. And it's well windy up here.'

'Wizz said it was the perfect place to chill. It's where we flew our kite when we were little.'

'Oh yeah,' says Clint. 'She told me about that.'

We cross the road and join the footpath on the other side. It's a bit late now, but I really wish I'd brought a coat.

'Well, that's all we need,' says Zofia, as a thick sea mist begins to wrap itself around us. 'How are we going to find her now?'

'I *think* the cliffs are that way,' I say, stumbling blindly across the damp grass. 'There was an old wooden seat where you could look out to sea.'

'Iiiiiiiiizie, where are you?' shouts Clint, edging slowly forward. 'We need to find her, Arch. Those cliffs are, like, four hundred feet high.'

And we walk round in circles, calling her name into the mist:

'IZZY, IZZY, WHERE ARE YOU, IZZY?'

Until I bash my leg against something. And the pain is so bad it stops me dead in my tracks. 'Urghh, what was that?'

'I think it's a sign,' says Zofia.

'You don't believe in stuff like that do you, Zoff?'

'No, I mean a wooden signpost,' she says, kneeling down to read it. 'Look.'

**DANGER CLIFF EDGE**

Clint's face is as white as snow. 'I'll never forgive myself if anything happens to her. She will be all right, won't she?'

'Yes, of course,' says Zofia. 'We'll find her, won't we, Archie?'

I try to sound like I really mean it. But the truth is, she could be anywhere.

'Definitely. She's up here somewhere, I'm sure she is.'

And I'm seriously thinking about telling Clint to call the police, when the sun cuts a hole in the mist and just for a second I'm pretty sure that I see someone. 'Over there, look!'

Clint howls her name into the wind. 'Izzer!'

Because there she is; about six feet in front of us, still as a statue, hands in pockets, her hair blowing in the wind.

‘Don’t move, babe,’ calls Clint. ‘You’re right near the edge.’

Me, Clint and Zofia join hands and inch slowly forward.

And I think I’m going to be sick.

‘Stay where you are,’ calls Clint. ‘We’re coming to get you.’

But my sister doesn’t sound all that pleased about it. ‘I thought I told you to leave me alone, Clinton.’

‘We were dead worried about you, babe. Weren’t we, Arch?’

‘Archie?’ she says, spitting out my name in disgust. ‘What’s he doing here? It was all his fault in the first place.’

I can just make out her ‘Izzy and Clinton 4 ever’ rucksack. In a few more steps, I might just be able to see the back of her head. ‘I’m really sorry about the photos, Izzy. I know I shouldn’t have done it, but I was so upset about Dinger.’

‘It’s true,’ says Zofia. ‘Archie’s really sorry.’

‘Who’s that?’ says Izzy. ‘Do I know you?’

‘I’m a friend of Archie’s. My name’s Zofia.’

‘Oh, so I’ve got an audience now,’ says Izzy. ‘Come to laugh at me like the rest of them, have you?’

Clint's face is a crumpled carpet of misery. 'Of course not, babe.'

'Leave me alone,' screams Izzy, lurching forward into the mist. 'I don't want to talk to you, OK?'

'What's that funny rushing sound?' says Zofia, squeezing my hand so hard that it hurts.

I squeeze back and try to stop my legs shaking. 'I'm not sure. But I think it's the sea breaking against the rocks.'

Clint lets out a frightened whimper and inches forward like a tightrope walker. 'You've got to believe me, Izzer. I'm not trying to get back with you or anything – you and Hamish are together now – I saw those photos and I just wanted to make sure you were OK.'

'Of course you don't want to get back with me,' says Izzy. 'Not now you've seen where we live.'

'Why would you even think that?' says Clint. 'I'd get back with you in a heartbeat if you'd have me. I love you, Izzer. And I couldn't care less where you live.'

'It's true,' says Zofia. 'He won't shut up about you. He wouldn't stop talking about you the whole bus journey.'

All I can see is the faint outline of my sister covered by a curtain of mist. 'Don't go any further, Wizz. You're really scaring me.'

Clint sounds like he can hardly breathe. 'Just turn round and walk toward us, babe. We're right behind you. Aren't we, guys?'

Me and Zofia manage to force out a frightened, 'Yes.'

But nothing happens.

'Izzer, *please*,' begs Clint. 'Don't do this to me, babe. You know I can't stand heights.'

All I can hear is the wind whistling and the waves crashing against the rocks below. It probably lasts for about thirty seconds, but it feels more like thirty years. That's the time it takes for my sister to put us out of our misery. And we all breathe a long sigh of relief as she reappears from out of the mist with the hint of a smile on her face.

'Do you really want to get back with me, Clinton?'

'You know I do, babe.'

'But we live in a hostel for homeless people,' says Izzy. 'You've seen the photos. It's a dump.'

'So what?' says Clint. 'It's not just about the

buildings, is it? It's about the people who live in them.'

Izzy takes Clint's hand. He pulls her towards him and wraps his arms around her. 'Don't you *ever* do that to me again.'

And me and Zofia look the other way while they lock lips – four times!

Clint looks like the cat that got the cat treats. 'So does this mean we're back together?'

Izzy seems pretty happy too. 'Looks like it.'

'And what about Hamish?'

Izzy hesitates. 'I made him up, Clinton … to stop you trying to find me. Sorry about that.'

'No, babe, that's bangin'. I hated thinking you were with someone else.'

But believe it or not, my sister hasn't finished apologising yet. 'And I'm sorry I was mean about Dinger, Archie. I miss him too.'

'Why, what happened to him?' says Clint.

'It's really unfair,' I say, suddenly remembering my epic fail at catnapping. 'We're not allowed pets at Manton House. So we had to take him to Mrs Watts' house.'

Clint obviously remembers her. 'You mean the mad cat lady?'

'That's right. And now she won't even let me come and visit!'

'Leave it with me, Arch,' says Clint. 'I might have an idea about that.'

'Like what?'

'Tell you later,' says Clint, checking his phone. 'Me and Izzer need to get back to school.'

But Izzy looks completely horrified. 'No way. I can't go back there now. Everyone's laughing at me.'

'No, they're not,' says Clint. 'Apart from Courtney, maybe.'

'I can't,' says Izzy. 'Maybe I could go to another school or something.'

Clint normally does exactly what my sister tells him. But just for once, he refuses to back down. 'No, I'm not having it. You've just got to be brave, babe. No one's going to laugh at you, I promise. And you can't hide away forever. Just tell them what it feels like and they'll understand.'

Izzy thinks about it for a *very* long time. 'OK, fine. But you'd better be right about this, Clinton.'

'We need to get back to school too, Archie,' says Zofia. 'If we don't to find that money by the end of the day, Callum will get the blame and there won't be a Leavers' Party.'

# 26

Mr Messy the caretaker is busy picking up litter and talking to himself as we race past him to the bottom of the field.

'Everything in its proper place, Lionel. Everything in its proper place.'

Zofia unhitches the gate to Mrs Goodall's conservation area and I follow her down the brown wood-chip path. 'Watch out for the stinging nettles.'

We pass poetry corner (a circle of logs with laminated poems on them) and the butterfly sanctuary (a patch of wild grass) and make our way towards the mindfulness hut.

'It's here somewhere. I know it is,' says Zofia, climbing into one of the old tyres hanging from the roof. 'Let's get out of the rain for a bit so we can think.'

'We haven't got much time,' I say, climbing into the tyre next to her and starting to swing. 'If we don't find it in the next twenty minutes the Leavers' Party will be cancelled.'

Zofia suddenly stops swinging. 'Wait a minute. Did you hear that?'

'What?'

'That scratching noise.'

And we both see it at the same time; the cardboard box in the corner beneath the dream catchers.

'Yessssss!' says Zofia, pumping her fist. 'You know what's inside it, don't you, Archie? It's Mr Blott's book safe, it has to be.'

I don't tell Zofia, but I'm not quite so optimistic. They say money talks, but since when did it make scratching noises?

'I wonder what the holes in the top are for?' says Zofia.

'Who cares?' I say. 'Open the box!'

Zofia slowly lifts the lid and we peer inside.

'…Oh.'

A small furry face is looking up at us.

'Oh no,' groans Zofia. 'I was expecting —'

'I don't believe it! It's Ronaldo.'

'Who?'

'Caitlin's guinea pig. She's had him since Year Four.'

'What the angry one, you mean?' says Zofia.

'The one she talked about in Star of the Week?'

'Yes. So you'd better be careful with him: he bites.'

'Oh … right,' says Zofia, her bottom lip starting to tremble.

For some reason, I'm actually quite relieved. Caitlin can be a bit thoughtless sometimes, but I never really believed she could be so mean.

'I suppose it's quite funny when you think about it. Caitlin wasn't talking about Callum. She was talking about her guinea pig.'

But Zofia obviously doesn't find it funny at all. She's sitting on the floor of the mindfulness hut with her head in her hands.

'You OK, Zoff?'

'Not really,' she sniffs. 'I thought being invisible could be cool for once. I thought we could prove Callum innocent and do something nice for the rest of the class. But it's all been a complete failure, hasn't it, Archie? We couldn't even get your cat back.'

'No, but we found my sister, didn't we? And we've still got' – I check my watch – 'thirteen-and-a-half minutes to work out who took that money. Come on, Zofia. What are we waiting for?'

'But we've tried all of 6B and practically everyone in Key Stage 2,' says Zofia. 'Who are we going to try next?'

'What about that quiet girl in Year Five who plays the recorder? Didn't Callum stick plasticine up the end of it?'

'He said he didn't do it,' says Zofia. 'But it's worth a try, I suppose.'

'Well, come on then,' I say, offering her my hand and helping her to her feet. 'We can still do this, Zofia. I know we can.'

# 27

Mrs Goodall is so busy talking to an angry parent about 'the unfortunate incident on the Swanage trip', that she doesn't notice the clicking mouse scurrying round in circles on her desk or the desperate search through the 'pupil progress' files on her old-fashioned monitor. But it only takes Zofia about two-and-a-half minutes to work out that the quiet girl in Year Five who plays the recorder has been off school for the last two weeks with chicken pox.

'Well, that's that then, isn't it?' she says. 'Come on, Archie. We might as well get the early bus.'

'Zoff, wait!' I say, following her down the corridor. 'We've still got time.'

But school is nearly over. Mr Messy is already pushing his cleaning trolley down the corridor, ready for the bell.

'Being invisible is the worst,' says Zofia. 'If people could see us, we might be able to convince them that Callum didn't do it.'

I check the clock at the end of the corridor. 'We've got six minutes. Come on, Zofia. There must be something we haven't thought of.'

'Like what?' she says, swerving to avoid a swarm of Year Four gymnasts who are about to walk straight through us. 'Everything we try is a complete disaster. And I thought it would be as easy as ABC!'

'Wait a minute. I've had an idea.' Maybe when I put it into words it will just sound ridiculous. But with five minutes and twenty seconds to the bell, it's the best that I've got. 'What if the person who took that money is someone like us?'

Zofia doesn't sound at all convinced. 'What, homeless, you mean?'

'No, invisible. Well, not invisible exactly, but the kind of person who can walk around the school all day without really being noticed.'

'Like who?'

I glance down the corridor at the man with the mop. 'Like a *caretaker*, for instance. Every morning at first break he does his rounds of the classrooms. Supposing he … supposing he…'

And that's when it hits me.

'As easy as ABC. Of *course*.'

'What *are* you talking about, Archie?'

But I've already started running. 'I think I know where the money is.'

'What are we doing in the library?' says Zofia. 'I thought you said you know where the money is.'

'I do,' I say, not feeling quite as confident as I walk towards the fiction section.

'I hope this isn't one of your jokes, Archie.'

I shake my head and start running my finger along the middle shelf. 'We watched him doing it, didn't we, Zoff? He goes round the school rounding up random piles of books and then puts them back on the shelves in alphabetical order.'

'Oh … right,' says Zofia. 'You mean…?'

'That's exactly what I mean.'

And there between *Little Women* and *Naughty Nancy Goes to School* is Mr Blott's book-safe version of *Les Miserables* with the party money in it.

# 28

We make it back to the classroom with about a minute to spare. Mr Messy is leaning outside on his mop, waiting eagerly for the bell to sound.

'We need to write a note first,' I say, tearing a page from my homework diary. 'To tell him what happened.' I scribble a few lines of explanation and hide Mr Blott's book safe under my sweatshirt. 'OK, Zoff. You ready for this?'

We walk down to the front of the class and take a seat on Mr Blott's desk, our legs dangling. I slip *Les Miserables* onto a pile of books and rest the note on top of it.

Zofia's smile is bright enough to light up a black hole. 'I can't wait to see their faces, can you?'

'Wish they could see ours too, though,' I say, staring out at my old classmates. 'I mean, it's not the same, is it?'

Mr Blott checks the clock on the wall. 'OK, guys, times up I'm afraid – unless anyone wants to tell me something about that missing party money.'

No one says a word – not even Callum Critchlow.

'That's what I thought,' says Mr Blott, looking almost as disappointed as everyone else in the class. 'Well, in that case, it looks like you're not going to get your Leavers' Party. What a sad way to end such an amazing year.'

'He hasn't seen it,' says Zofia. 'What are we going to do?'

There's only one thing I *can* do. I reach across and push *Les Miserables* off the side of the desk. It lands on the floor with a loud thud.

'Be quiet!' says Mr Blott. 'This isn't funny, you know.'

And then he sees it.

'Wait a minute. How did *that* get there?'

Zofia starts clapping, like it's the end of the play. 'Well done, Archie. This is brilliant.'

'What is it?' calls Callum.

'It's the money for the Leavers' Party,' says Mr Blott, opening the front cover and checking inside.

'Told you I didn't take it,' says Callum.

Mr Blott still looks mystified. 'But I've looked everywhere. How did it get down there?'

And the whole class is so gobsmacked that no one moves a muscle when the bell goes.

'Someone's left you a note, Mr Blott,' says Caitlin, handing him the torn-out page from my homework diary. 'I think you'd better have a look at it.'

It ought to explain everything. But when he finishes reading, Mr Blott still looks completely mystified.

Caitlin has her hand up. 'What does it say? And who's it from?'

Mr Blott shakes his head and begins to read it to us: '*Dear Mr Blott, Callum didn't take the money for The Leavers' Party. We found it in the library.*'

'Oh yeah,' says Caitlin. 'So who put it there?'

'It was me,' says a voice.

Everyone looks round, trying to work out where the voice came from. Because no one has noticed the man with the mop, who's been listening quietly at the door. Mr Messy walks to the front of the class. 'If you don't mind me saying so, Mr Blott, your classroom is a tad on the messy side.'

'It's true,' says Callum. 'You're a wicked teacher, but you should definitely keep your desk more tidy.'

Mr Messy nods in agreement. 'Everything in its proper place, that's my motto. So when I took that book back to the library, I naturally thought I was doing you a favour. How was I to know there was money in it?'

'That's true, Lionel,' says Mr Blott. 'And thank you for letting me know.'

'That's quite all right,' says Mr Messy, grabbing his mop and heading back to the corridor. 'And now if you'll excuse me, I've got work to do.'

Caitlin has her hand up. 'Please can I say something, Mr Blott?'

'What is it, Caitlin?'

'I'm sorry I told everyone you took that money, Callum. I know it was mean of me, but I've been having some terrible problems with my guinea pig.'

'No worries,' says Callum, who looks like he's forgotten already. 'We all make mistakes sometimes – even me!'

And everyone laughs.

'Well, that's good, Archie,' says Zofia. 'It looks like our work here is done.'

'Yes,' I say, knowing I should feel happy, but not quite managing to. 'It would be nice if we could join in, though.'

The only person in the classroom not laughing is Mr Blott. In fact, he looks extremely confused. 'Wait a minute 6B. I haven't finished reading yet. Listen to this: *So have a great Leavers' Party. And we hope you really enjoy the massive water fight. Yours sincerely, Zofia Kieslowski and Archie Ebbs.*'

'Who are Zofia Kieslowski and Archie Ebbs?' says a voice from the back.

'Don't be silly,' says Callum. 'Zofia is an awesome Polish girl who can say goodbye in seven different languages.'

'It's true,' blushes Zofia. 'I can.'

'And Ebbo is, like, the funniest kid I know. You must remember: *I'm going to wash my hair with poo tonight. I've been washing it with shampoo for years. Just think how good it's going to look when I use the real thing!*'

A ripple of knowing laughter circles the classroom.

'Yeah, very funny, Archie,' says Zofia.

It might not be a very good joke, but it seems to have jogged people's memories.

'Archie was my friend,' says Josh.

'We used to make films together,' says Amir.

'I went round to his old house in Station Road,' says Caitlin. 'But there was a For Sale sign up and no one was in.'

Mr Blott runs his hand through his cool spiky hair. 'And Zofia did some of the best creative writing I've ever seen from a Year Six. I wonder where they've been?'

Being invisible is bad enough. But just sitting here while they say nice things about me is the worst agony of all. And I know it's pointless, but I can't stop myself jumping off Mr Blott's desk and trying to join in.

'It's all right,' I say, hoping to win them over with the fakest of fake smiles. 'I've just been on holiday, that's all.'

Zofia jumps down with me and grabs my hand. 'What are you doing, Archie?'

'They've started to remember us, Zofia. Maybe if I talk to them, I can make them see us again.'

Zofia doesn't sound very optimistic. 'If you say so.'

'Yeah, it was really cool actually,' I continue, trying desperately to grab their attention. 'My mum took me and Izzy on a world cruise.'

But not one face is looking in my direction.

'Stop it, Archie,' says Zofia. 'Why are you saying all this?'

'You *know* why. Because I don't want tell them about Manton House.'

'Yeah, I get it,' says Zofia. 'But if they're really your friends they won't care.'

'They can't see me anyway. So what's the point?'

Zofia smiles and squeezes my hand. 'Well, it's better than lying, isn't it? And you remember what Clint said: *you've just got to be brave*. Come on, Archie. Tell them what it feels like and they might even understand.'

I don't know where the words come from, but having Zofia standing right next to me probably helps. It doesn't even sound like my voice to begin with. All I know is that it needs to be said.

'I never thought it could happen to a family like mine. But a few months ago, we got evicted from our old house. That's why there was a For Sale sign up, Caitlin. Mum tried to find us somewhere else, but we couldn't afford anywhere, so they sent us to a bed and breakfast hostel for homeless people. That's where I met Zofia.'

'But it's not like a bed and breakfast you stay in on your holidays,' says Zofia. 'It's like one tiny room with, like, three beds in it and you have to share a toilet. And it's only supposed to be temporary. But we've been living there for nearly six months.'

At first, I think I'm imagining it. But I can't be because even Callum is sitting up and paying attention.

'Zofia, Zofia! Look!'

*Every* head in the classroom has turned in our direction.

'That's amazing,' says Zofia. 'Keep going, Archie. I think they can hear us.'

No one moves, so I just keep talking. 'It's really horrible. I can't sleep because it's so noisy. There's no wifi and you're not even allowed to have pets. That's why I'm always so tired. And that's why I've never told anyone. I was really scared that you'd make fun of me or something.'

I'm not exactly sure when they started seeing us. But the bell went five minutes ago, and I suddenly realise that the only reason the whole class is still sitting there is because they're listening carefully to every word I say.

And after being invisible for all this time, you have no idea how good it feels. Zofia tells them about her sister's nightmares and the mould on the wall. And I tell them about the telly that only gets one channel, how quickly you get fed up with takeaways and what it feels like to be covered in bed-bug bites.

But the best moment of all is when practically everyone in 6B starts shouting out questions.

'No toilet! What do you do if you're really desperate?'

'What happened to Dinger?'

'How do you say goodbye in Japanese?'

'How do you cook anything if there isn't an oven?'

'What's your favourite takeaway?'

'What do you do all night if there's no wifi?'

Mr Blott claps his hands. 'All right, guys. I think that's enough questions for today. Thank you, Zofia. Thank you, Archie. That was extremely brave of you. I'm proud of you both.'

'I still don't really get it,' I say, as we celebrate our reappearance with a packet of Haribos at the bus stop. 'Why do you reckon they can see us again?'

'Not sure,' says Zofia. 'But we told them what it felt like – living at Manton House, I mean. Maybe it's because people can see you more clearly if they understand how you feel.'

'Or maybe it's because we found the party money.'

'Yeah … maybe. Feels great through, doesn't it?' says Zofia, biting the head off a gummy bear.

But a horrible thought has just popped into mine. 'What if it doesn't last? What if they can't see us tomorrow? What if no one can see us *now*?'

The bus doors open and we race up the steps.

And I've never been so relieved to be shouted at.

'Oi, you two, where do you think you're going?' bellows the bus driver. 'And I don't know what you're smiling at, sonny, because it's not funny, believe me.' He reaches across the ticket machine with his palm outstretched. 'Now let's see your bus passes, shall we?'

## 29

It looks like Mum has made a real effort. She's changed out of her uniform and even microwaved us some baked potatoes.

'I'm sorry, guys,' she says, as all three of us squeeze into the armchair together and pretend to watch *Sharon and Mark's Tanzanite Spectacular*. 'I've been thinking about what you said the other night, Archie. And you were right.'

'It's OK, Mum.'

'No, it's not OK. You and Izzy needed me and I haven't been there for you.'

Izzy puts her arm around her and strokes her hair. 'Please don't cry, Mum.'

'And I'm sorry that Mrs Watts won't let you see Dinger, Archie. I'm sure he's missing you.'

'That's OK, Mum. He didn't look *that* unhappy.'

She looks up at the ceiling, like she's trying to tip thc tcars back into her eyes. 'I know I haven't been myself lately. I might need a bit of help from somewhere, but that's going to change, I promise. And I haven't given up, guys. I'll get you out of here if it's the last thing I—'

Someone is banging on the door.

'Don't answer it,' says Mum. 'It could be anyone.'

'It's all right, I'll get it,' says Izzy, jumping up excitedly and messing about with her hair. 'It's only Clint.'

'Really?' says Mum. 'I didn't think you wanted him to know about this place.'

'I didn't,' says Izzy. 'But I've told everyone at school now and they were all really cool about it – apart from Courtney Stupid Foden, of course.'

Clint rips off his beanie and out bursts his curly hair. 'All right, babe? All right, Archie? All right, Mrs E?'

'Hello Clint,' says Mum, almost managing a smile. 'And how are things with you?'

He's checking out the beds and the stains on the wall. 'Yeah, yeah, bangin' thanks, Mrs E.'

'Well, it's lovely to see you again,' says Mum. 'And we've certainly missed your cooking, haven't we, guys?'

'Which reminds me,' says Clint, taking a

plastic container from his 'Clint Hearts Izzy' rucksack and handing it to me. 'I've got a little present for the Archmeister here – for helping me out on the cliffs.'

'Cliffs? What cliffs!' says Mum.

Izzy gives Clint one of her 'special' looks. 'Nothing, Mum. It's for Clinton's art project. Archie's going to draw the cliffs for him – isn't that right, Arch?'

I nod unconvincingly and take off the lid of the plastic container. And my mouth is watering already. Because inside are two whole layers of Clinton's Bangin' Chocolate Brownies.

'Wicked! Thanks, Clint.'

'What about the other thing, babe?' says Izzy, mysteriously. 'Did you speak to your mum?'

'I did as it happens,' says Clint with an enormous smile. 'And it's all sorted. Mum says Dinger can stay at our place until you find somewhere permanent. And you can come and visit him whenever you like, Arch.' He offers me his fist to bump. 'That's if it's cool with you, Mrs E.'

Mum looks a bit doubtful. 'And you're quite sure your mother's happy about this, Clint?'

'Yeah, deffo. She said she'd enjoy having him.'

'Please, Mum,' I say, my face already full of bangin' brownie. 'It's not fair that I'm not allowed to see him.'

Mum thinks for a bit. 'Well, I'd have to speak to Mrs Watts first.'

I grab her phone and hand it to her. 'Do it now, Mum, *please*.'

'All right, all right,' she says, scrolling through her contacts list. 'Just let me think what to say to her first.'

'Well, there is one thing you should probably tell her, Mum.'

'What's that, Archie?'

'You should tell her to keep her back door locked.'

# 30

'Before I shoot you, Archie, there's something I want to say first.'

Mr Blott puts down his Giant Super-Soaker. I put down my water pistol.

'It's not about the talent show, is it? Didn't you like my jokes?'

'The jokes were wicked, Archie – especially the one about eating clocks.' (*It's rather time consuming.*) 'And thanks for being such an excellent compere.'

The inflatable assault course is awesome by the way. We're sitting at the top of the slide while all around us a massive water fight is raging. Callum and Caitlin are pelting Josh with wet sponges and Zofia and Amir are taking it in turns to throw buckets of water at each other as they swing through the blow-up palm trees. Everyone looks like they're having the time of their lives – even Mr Messy who's waiting patiently by the generator and probably dreaming of the after-party clear-up operation.

And I can't wait to join in again. Unfortunately, my favourite teacher has a rather serious look on his face.

'So what did you want to say to me, Mr Blott?'

He runs his hand through his wet spikeless hair. 'I feel like I let you down, Archie.'

'What do mean?'

'I spoke to your mum,' he says. 'We had a really good chat.'

'Oh … right.'

'I should have seen what you were going through, Archie. I had a feeling something was wrong.'

'Don't worry, you couldn't have seen anyway.' (We've talked about this. And me and Zofia both agree that it would be extremely unwise to tell *anyone* about turning invisible.) 'I mean, I didn't want people to know.'

'Well … anyway,' says Mr Blott, ducking to avoid a shower of water bombs. 'The school will be writing letters of support for you and Zofia to the housing department. And I want you to promise me that if anything like this ever happens to you again, you won't keep it bottled up inside.'

I'm so desperate to get back to the water fight that I don't even hesitate. 'I promise.'

'Good,' says Mr Blott, reaching for his Giant Super Soaker. 'OK Archie. I'll give you five seconds to get away. And then I'm going to shoot!'

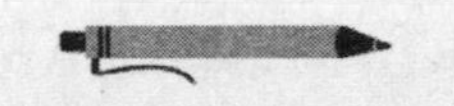

After we've dried off, we all go back to the hall for pizza and smoothies. Mrs Goodall wishes us luck at our new schools, at least half of us have to pretend we've got soap in our eyes, and Mr Blott says we're the best class he's ever had. According to Izzy he said exactly the same thing when *she* left, so maybe he says it every year.

And it's starting to feel like old times.

Caitlin is boasting about the greatest goals she's ever scored.

Josh wants to know how many zombies I've killed.

Plus, it looks like Top Table Productions is back in business.

And I've got admit, I'm pretty happy about it. Even so, I'll never forget how lonely it feels to be invisible.

'There's a sleepover at my place on Saturday, Archie,' says Caitlin. 'We're playing Fortnite for the first five hours and then we're going to watch a movie.'

It's not that I don't want to be friends with them, but it's probably going to take a little bit longer to get back to the way we were. 'Sorry guys, I'm busy on Saturday. Zofia and I are going to Callum's house. But how about *next* week?"

'Yeah cool,' says Josh. 'I really want to show you the Awesomeopolis theme park. It's called "Awesome Towers".'

'Why don't you come too, Zofia?' says Caitlin. 'That's if you want to, of course.'

Zofia looks a bit surprised – but in a good way. 'Yes … great … thanks.'

'We're going to start work on a new movie,' says Amir. 'It's called *The Last Beetroot*. What do you think, Archie?

And I'm just about to crack my favourite beetroot joke when I suddenly remember one of the first things that Zofia said to me: *you don't have to be funny the whole time to make people like you, Archie.*

So I just smile and say: 'Yes, nice one, guys. I can't wait.'

## Nine Months Later

OK, so it's taken a bit longer than we all expected, but now that we're here it was definitely worth the wait.

Mum bombarded the council with phone calls and emails until they moved us into another B&B – and then *another* where Izzy could have her own room. But it wasn't until last month that we finally got the letter from the housing association saying that our new flat was ready.

And three days ago, we moved in!

As you can see, it's what Clint would call a 'pretty sweet gaff'. I'm not going to give you a guided tour, but I've got my own bedroom (which is really cool, by the way), there are solar panels on the roof and a little place out the back where you can play football.

But perhaps I should fill you in on some of the other stuff that's happened since you last saw me. For a start, I haven't turned invisible again. I did feel a bit invisible when I started secondary school. But Izzy said everyone felt like that for the first few weeks. And it was even better after me and Zoff signed up for junior choir and coding club.

Ronaldo is alive and well and living at … Caitlin's house. Her mum told her she would never have tried to get rid of him. She just wanted her to clean out his cage now and then.

'Oi, Ebbo,' says Callum. 'Is it ready yet, I'm starving?'

'Patience, my friend,' says Clint, who's strutting around the new kitchen in his REAL MEN COOK apron. 'We've got to wait for you know who.'

'Oh yeah,' says Cal, who's made all it all the way to the Easter holidays without being excluded once. 'When's he coming?'

'Soon,' says Zofia. 'Can't wait to see him, can you, Cait?'

Caitlin and Zofia have been whispering about 'girl stuff' on the sofa. Funny how those two are best mates now.

'OK, everyone,' says Amir, who's filming the whole thing for his new documentary. 'I think they're coming. Try to act naturally, OK?'

So Josh starts doing his robot dance!

But you're probably wondering why all my friends from school are here. Well, that's easy. Today is special. That's why Clint's vegan spaghetti for ten is bubbling away nicely and Izzy (yes Izzy!) has baked a cake with 'Welcome Home' on it.

And this must be the guest of honour.

A key turns in the lock and everyone cheers as Mum pushes open the door. 'Oh my goodness. We have got a house full.'

I certainly don't want to cry in front of all my friends. But I have to admit, there's definitely a tear in my eye when Mum opens the door of the cat carrier and…

And…

And…

And out steps Dinger.

# Acknowledgements

With huge thanks to the wonderful team at Firefly Press. To my agent Anne Clark for her superb eye for detail and unwavering support. To Ken and Emma at Horsham Matters and Kamila Kowalski at the Polish Saturday School for helping me with my research. To our cat, Pax, a shoo-in for the part of Dinger in the movie. And last, but never least, my wife Deborah, for more than I could ever say.

If you want to learn more about homelessness, the Shelter website (https://www.shelter.org.uk/) is excellent and my local charity Turning Tides (https://www.turning-tides.org.uk/) does some really great work on the south coast.